To James.

Happy Christmas 2005.

D1098976

Alex Mabon was born in the Highlands of Scotland in 1939. On completion of schooling in Inverness, he had a brief spell in Journalism before enlisting in the Royal Air Force where he served for ten years. During this time he travelled extensively in the Middle East and the Far East.

On leaving the RAF, he was employed in various positions. This culminated in twenty years in commercial property business continuity management in the City of London.

He is now retired and lives in Kent.

His first novel, 'The Lads from the Ferry' was published in 2004.

THE BATTLE
OF THE FERRY

Alex Mabon

The Battle
Of The Ferry

Pegasus

PEGASUS PAPERBACK

© Copyright 2005
Alex Mabon

The right of Alex Mabon to be identified as author of
this work has been asserted by him in accordance with the
Copyright, Designs and Patents Act 1988

All Rights Reserved

No reproduction, copy or transmission of this publication
may be made without written permission.
No paragraph of this publication may be reproduced,
copied or transmitted save with the written permission of the
publisher, or in accordance with the provisions
of the Copyright Act 1956 (as amended).

Any person who does any unauthorised act in relation to
this publication may be liable to criminal
prosecution and civil claims for damage.

A CIP catalogue record for this title is
available from the British Library

ISBN 1 903490 16 2

Pegasus is an imprint of
Pegasus Elliot MacKenzie Publishers Ltd.
www.pegasuspublishers.com

First Published in 2005

Pegasus
Sheraton House Castle Park
Cambridge England

Printed & Bound in Great Britain

DEDICATIONS

With grateful thanks to Dr. David Brennand-Roper, MA., FRCP., Mr Christopher Blauth MS., FRCS., and the doctors and nursing staff in the Intensive Care Unit, High Dependency Unit and Cardiac Ward of London Bridge Hospital. Without their skills this book would probably not have been written.
Well – the author has to blame someone.

By the same author:-

The Lads From The Ferry

From the tough and impoverished Ferry district of Inverness during the dark days of the second world war a group of youngsters emerge. The friendships made whilst growing up in the close-knit community survive a life-time. John Urquhart and his best mate Sandy Roberts cause mayhem from primary school right through adolescence and into early manhood in the R.A.F. in their desperate attempts to find a girl-friend - any girl-friend.

Life is a constant struggle, with the down-trodden Ferry folk on one side battling with the posh people from "up the Hill" and the Highland Constabulary.

Even the grown ups from the Ferry create problems. With people like Jocky Winngate, the father of most of the Ferry kids, and one of his illegitimate twin daughters Marie Winngate, who runs massage parlours and operates scams under several aliases, it is hardly surprising that the Chief Constable is a secret transvestite.

But Jocky Winngate's chickens come home to roost on a cold wet morning in April 1962 when he receives a summons to attend the local police station where two women are being held in custody. Women who have all the appearances of being his daughters.

The story continues.

PROLOGUE

BERKSHIRE, ENGLAND.

Lady Marie Castello looked out of the window of her manor house. Standing in the Blue Room she stared across the sprawling grounds of her Berkshire estate. It was a typical balmy early summer day. Overhead a jet aircraft could be seen against a blue sky. It was a far cry from the council estate background of her childhood in Inverness.

She shook herself, almost as though warding off some ghostly presence. Lifting a hand-bell to summon her butler she looked again at the photograph she had found earlier that day whilst searching through some old papers.

Her butler approached.

"Tea, my Lady?" he asked.

"Brandy," replied Lady Castello, "and bring a large one."

The butler looked at her in amazement. He had been working for Lady Castello for fourteen years and had been with Lord Castello for five years prior to that. His Lordship's death from drowning had occurred shortly after the mismatched pair had married. The police had reached no conclusion as to why Lord Castello had been in his swimming pool at three o'clock in the morning, totally naked. But the butler knew that Lady Castello was aware exactly what His Lordship had been doing in the swimming pool as she had been at the pool at the time. As a result of this he was very wary of Lady Castello.

In the long time that the butler had known the mistress of the house, he had never seen her drink brandy at ten o'clock in the morning. Champagne - but never brandy.

"Are you all right, madam?" he asked, looking at Lady Castello, who was standing transfixed, staring at an old photograph.

"What? Oh yes I'm fine. Just get me that brandy. On second

13

thoughts, bring me a bottle."

"Certainly Madam. May I remind you that the Lord Lieutenant is due in an hour to discuss the arrangements for the royal visit?"

Lady Castello waved her hand in dismissal. She had other things on her mind.

The butler departed. Not with any great haste. At seventy years of age he had already done his fair share of rushing.

"Doddering old fool," muttered Lady Castello looking at the retreating butler.

She looked at the photograph again. The black and white picture was curled around the edges but the subject of the photograph was clearly visible. It was of an alfresco party. Not the type of alfresco function Lady Castello had become accustomed to attending. Glyndebourne, Royal Ascot, and Wimbledon, were not complete without her presence.

The photograph depicted a street scene. Red white and blue bunting and Union Flags hung from broken wooden fencing and houses located on the fringe of the photograph. The missing pieces of fencing could be seen on a bonfire in the foreground of the picture. What appeared to be a garden shed and broken furniture added to the conflagration. Trestle tables, covered with what were obviously bed sheets, were laden with food and drink.

The thirty adults in the small snap, predominately women, seemed to be suffering from some form of madness. A further glance at the picture revealed the reason for this. It was not some form of palsy. It was a combination of euphoria and drink. Testimony to this was the empty bottles of VP wine scattered on the tables amidst the jelly and cakes which were being consumed by a large number of children.

She looked again at the faces in the photograph. A wave of nostalgia hit her. Where had the years gone? Almost sixty years had elapsed since the scene depicted had taken place.

But there was no doubting the occasion or the location. She could see the street sign on the corner house which read "South Drive". She could see the banners proclaiming "VE Day Party". The war in Europe had ended. It was May 1945 and the residents of the Ferry district of Inverness were celebrating.

She saw her father Jocky with his arms around two of the

young daughters of one of their neighbours. Standing close to her father she recognised a face she had not thought about for many years. John Urquhart, the little sod she had grown up with in childhood. The same John Urquhart who had nearly got her imprisoned in 1962, following a riot and fire at their primary school re-union in Inverness. Standing beside him, recognisable despite the fact that he was only five years old at the time the photograph was taken, was Urquhart's mate Sandy Roberts.

Lady Costello looked at the young version of herself standing in the foreground of the picture looking straight at the camera. Next to her was Violet MacDonald. Violet had a strange look on her face. It was almost as though she was afraid of the camera.

She recalled the interview at Inverness police station following her arrest at the school re-union in 1962. The police had called there to arrest John Urquhart. However when one of the police officers recognised her from the Most Wanted list displayed at the police station she had been arrested instead of Urquhart.

It had been a stroke of luck that, when being questioned, she had recognised the Chief Constable from a photograph which he had sent her when he had written to her two years earlier.

Had it not been for the fact that she knew the Chief Constable, she had no doubt that she would have spent a long time in Holloway Prison. No wonder the other police officers had looked bemused when the Chief Constable had stopped the questioning on "grounds of National Security."

Lady Castello reflected on her life since then. She was now a very successful businesswoman and part of the trendy London and New York social scene. With four marriages behind her, she was also a very wealthy woman. It was no coincidence that, apart from her first husband, all her husbands had been extremely wealthy and in their eighties.

The butler approached with the brandy. She dismissed him. She was quite capable of pouring a drink. She had enough experience.

She raised her glass.

"I think it's time we met again," she muttered to herself,

looking at the photograph of John Urquhart.

She re-read the article in the Inverness Herald. She had subscribed to the newspaper for over forty years, ever since she had taken a business interest in the less salubrious drinking establishments in the town. The previous day she had returned from a three month business trip to the Far East. Three months' editions of The Herald were awaiting her perusal. She had only got as far as reading the newspaper on top of the pile, which happened to be that week's edition.

It was the article about a re-union of former Kessock School pupils that had caught her eye. It was this that had prompted her to search through her old papers.

She took another sip of brandy.

Her mind was made up. She would attend the school re-union.

She would visit Inverness in the hope of seeing John Urquhart and Sandy Roberts. Although she still had a score to settle with them she had a sneaking admiration for the pair. She realised that no harm had been intended in their interferences over the years. Who knows - it may even be that the real love of her life would be at the re-union, the little lad who stood beside her in the old photograph. Her first ever kiss.

But if Lady Castello had continued reading through her back copies of The Herald, she would have realised that one half of the Urquhart and Roberts partnership was in a place where even she could not reach him, despite all her money and influence.

CHAPTER ONE

APRIL 1962

INVERNESS

The Chief Constable was almost running as he entered the police station. He could hardly believe the news. Two of the most wanted criminals in the history of the Highland Constabulary were being detained in his station. One of them, John Urquhart, was the chief suspect in an incident involving injury to a police dog at a riot at the Kessock primary school sports day seventeen years earlier, and was now apparently involved in the incident which had just totally destroyed the same school by fire. Urquhart also appeared to have some criminal involvement with Marie Winngate, one of the most prolific con artists in Britain, who was also being held in custody.

Bizarrely however there were now two women in the station who appeared to be Marie Winngate. The second woman had been arrested several days earlier in the Crown district of the town. She was the spitting image of the Marie Winngate arrested at the school re-union.

The Chief Constable entered the interview room as Chief Inspector Berk was interviewing John Urquhart. The Chief Constable took one look at Urquhart. Definitely a criminal. The Chief Constable had seen all types. Urquhart looked timid enough. But then again so had Hitler in his early twenties.

The Chief Constable had no opportunity to see either of the women held in custody before Probationary Police Constable David Thomson spotted the coincidence. On checking the custody records he noticed that the two women, Marie Winngate and Alison Forbes, had the same birthday.

The explanation was obvious. They were twins.

The Chief Constable recollected Marie Winngate's father. Jocky Winngate had been a source of irritation to the police for some time. Nothing specific, but he was from the Ferry area of the town. That was enough reason to be suspicious.

"I think we had better bring in Mr.Winngate for questioning," the Chief Constable commanded. "This may be our opportunity to pin something on him.

Jocky Winngate was working at Jock's Kitchen supervising the weekly production of gruel for the town's school pupils when the police car arrived for him. To jeers from his fellow workers he was bundled into the car.

Jocky walked into the police station expecting the worst. He had seen the article and picture in the local newspaper two days earlier stating that the police had a prisoner in custody. He was certain that the woman in the photograph was his daughter Marie. He had not seen her for several years.

A few minutes later Jocky walked into the interview room to be confronted by two identical looking women.

"Do you know either of these two women?" the Chief Constable asked Jocky.

Jocky looked at Marie Winngate and Alison Forbes.

"Yes," he replied, "they are my twin daughters."

Alison looked at Jocky. At five feet two inches in height and nine stone in weight he was not the image she had always carried of her father. A father she thought had died before she had been born.

Alison fainted.

Marie looked at Jocky and then at the Chief Constable.

"I wish to make a statement," she stated, "but only to the Chief Constable."

The Chief Constable, seeing the possibility of closing the arrests and locking up John Urquhart and Marie Winngate for a long time, agreed to the request for a private meeting.

The others departed the room leaving the Chief Constable and Marie facing each other.

"Do you know Lucy Chalmers?" was the surprise opener from Marie.

The Chief Constable blinked. Lucy Chalmers? How the hell

did Marie Winngate know about Lucy Chalmers? He had been writing to Lucy secretly swapping tales of lust and depravity. He had even sent her a photograph of himself wearing a policewoman's uniform complete with suspenders and a blonde wig.

Marie looked at the Chief Constable and smiled.

Realisation dawned on the Chief Constable.

"You?" he asked in a shaky voice.

Five minutes later the Chief Constable advised an astonished Chief Inspector that all parties were to be released. There would be no charges "on grounds of National Security."

.

CHAPTER TWO

APRIL 1962

INVERNESS

John Urquhart walked out of the police station located at Inverness Castle. He could scarcely believe the turn of events over the previous few days. He had reported to the police station on discharge from hospital following the fracas at the Kessock school reunion. Whilst in hospital he had been visited by Susan Simpson, his long lost soul mate from infant school days.

He pondered on the events of the previous hour. The interview at the police station had been strange. He had been asked to identify his one time girl-friend Alison Forbes. He had then been confronted by an identical looking female. It transpired that the second girl was an old pen friend of his, Marie Winngate, the twin sister of Alison. Neither of the girls had been aware of the existence of the other. Jocky Winngate had also been at the police station "helping the police with their enquiries". Charges of fraud against Marie and the threat of charges against himself had been dropped on the instructions of the Chief Constable with no sensible explanation.

As John left the police station he observed a very sheepish Jocky being lambasted by his new found daughters.

John entered the telephone box at the foot of the steps leading to the castle. He inserted two penny pieces and dialled Susan's number in Edinburgh. He waited nervously as the telephone rang at the other end. On hearing Susan's voice his heart pounded.

On the train taking him back to his R.A.F. station in London John reflected on his brief telephone conversation with Susan. Clutched in his hand was the note she had written to him whilst he had been in hospital. A note which expressed feelings that she had felt since they had both been children. Feelings shared by John.

At long last he had a real girl-friend. He could now forget about Alison Forbes. He could even forget about Lesley Graham, the nurse he had written to almost every day for a year whilst he had been in the Libyan Desert. He could not get over the shock when he had realised that Lesley - the girl, was in fact Leslie - a boy. The whole farce of his writing to a male nurse for over a year had been at the instigation of his elder brother James, in retribution for pranks John had played over a period of years.

He could not get his head around the fact that his one time pen friend Jessica Rawlings, an exotic dancer from Glasgow, was in reality the Marie Winngate he had just seen in the police station. The same Marie he had been in primary school with.

But John did not realise that Marie Winngate was a woman not to be trifled with. Even as Marie stood outside Inverness nick she was planning her revenge on John. For good measure she would also crucify his mate Sandy Roberts who was equally to blame for her current misfortunes. The torrent of abuse she was heaping on her father Jocky and her new found sister Alison only served to fuel her wish for vengeance.

She decided that John Urquhart and Sandy Roberts would be punished.

No matter how long it took.

CHAPTER THREE

APRIL 1962

INVERNESS

After ten minutes of abuse from Marie, and tears from Alison, Jocky Winngate had had enough. He ran from the police station, heading for the MacEwans Arms in Grant Street. He had to get away from his twin daughters.

Not that these were Jocky's only children. He had no idea of the precise number of children he had sired. He knew of a further seven scattered throughout the U.K. but he felt sure there were others. It was not that he did not believe in contraception. Things just happened too fast when he was around women.

He was aware of the location of only two of his male offspring. Their internment in the local Porterfield Prison had been widely publicised. They were both serving a two year prison sentence for bank robbery. A robbery that had gone spectacularly wrong when the vehicle they had used as a getaway car had run out of fuel one hundred yards from the bank, and just outside the police station. Had they any sense they would have run with the money. Instead of running they choose to brawl in the street blaming each other for the lack of fuel. The noise had quickly brought three burly constables out of the station, all of them only partially dressed as they had been in the middle of their weekly ballet dance instruction.

The lads, Robbie Nelson aged 23 and Terry Nelson aged 21, had the same mother but had no idea that Jocky was their father. But then again Mr. Nelson had no idea that Jocky was the real father.

Robbie and Terry had been incarcerated for twenty three months. With no time off for good behaviour their release was imminent.

Over his third pint of Heavy followed by whisky chasers Jocky reflected on where he had gone wrong in life. His job as supervisor at Jock's Kitchen was secure. He had been there for thirty one years, since the age of fourteen when he had been expelled from the High School for having had a relationship with the games mistress. He had never married. He had no need to. Despite his diminutive stature he had no end of success with the ladies. He had a charisma which brought out the worst in women at any time.

He recalled the time, in 1938, when a Schools Health Inspector had called to inspect Jock's Kitchen. The inspector, a toffee-nosed girl not much older than him, had only been in his company fifteen minutes when she came under his spell and fell pregnant. The twin daughters he had just seen at the police station were proof of this liaison. He and the Health Inspector, he never could remember her name, had decided that the sisters should be unaware of each others existence. As a consequence Marie had lived with Jocky and the other daughter was brought up by her mother.

At the age of eight Marie left Inverness to stay with an aunt in Glasgow. The relocation was on the advice of the police and on the insistence of the education authorities who could not cope with her. Jocky had seen Marie on only a few occasions since then. He was amazed at the criminal skills she had acquired in the fifteen years absence. Heaven knows how she had managed to wangle herself out of this latest escapade.

Lifting his Bells, he raised a glass to the twins. A smile came over his face as he reflected on how successful Marie had become. She was probably one of the top con-artists in Britain. As for the other one, Alison, well she was a right stuck up little cow.

Lowering his glass he reflected on the main cause of his problems to date. One word summoned it up. Women!

There and then he decided he was finished with women.

Two nips of Bells later he caught the eye of the young barmaid. It was her first day on the job. She was young enough to be his daughter.

Fifteen minutes later Jocky and the barmaid were in his

23

poky little flat above a chip shop two doors away from the pub.

A further fifteen minutes found him back in the bar being served free whisky by a very flustered young barmaid.

Jocky wondered if he would ever see Marie or Alison again.

CHAPTER FOUR

APRIL 1962

LONDON

Senior Aircraftsman Sandy Roberts was on guard duty on the main gate at R.A.F Northolt. It was a Friday morning. He had been in Inverness with John Urquhart earlier that week but as he was not required at the police station he had arrived back at Northolt three days earlier. His guard duty had been prompted by an I.R.A. scare in the London area.

He posed no deterrent to would-be terrorists as he lounged in an easy chair on the verandah of the guard-room, his Lee Enfield .303 rifle laying across his lap. It was not a normal Friday. It was Easter week-end and as far as Sandy was concerned that meant that the camp had closed down and all persons of Irish descent were in church.

Detecting a movement out of the corner of one eye (the other eye was glued to a copy of Men Only magazine) Sandy arose in panic and promptly fell off his chair, his rifle clattering to the ground.

A pseudo Irish voice, from a figure standing behind him, whispered in his ear.

"Give us a kiss, darling," the voice said.

"For God's sake, Johnny, I could have killed you," Sandy retorted, struggling to rise as his foot was wrapped around the rifle sling.

"What a way to go," replied John, "thrashed to death with a girlie magazine."

The following ten minutes were spent discussing the events of the previous week in Inverness.

They agreed that never seeing Marie Winngate again would

be no bad thing.

Ten days later they received notification of a posting to the Far East. Trouble had erupted on the borders between Indonesia and Borneo. Someone at the Air Ministry in London, clearly with a sense of humour, had decided that Corporal Urquhart and Senior Aircraftsman Roberts were required in Singapore to bolster the British defences. Due to the urgency in the posting there was no time for leave. A phone call to their next of kin and loved ones would have to suffice.

John's call was received by a very tearful Susan in Edinburgh.

Sandy had to be content with a call to his parents. He was still having trouble finding a girl-friend.

In the last week of April 1962 John and Sandy arrived on Singapore Island.

Two days after arrival they were ensconced in the depths of a top-secret joint services establishment located at R.A.F. Changi. Working alongside other R.A.F., Royal Navy and British Army personnel, they were part of an elite team co-ordinating the war against terrorism.

Their upbringing in the tough Ferry district and tuition at the "Kessie" Primary School made them ideally qualified for the task.

CHAPTER FIVE

DECEMBER 1962

INVERNESS

Violet MacDonald opened her eyes. It was a special day. She knew that it was a special day because her nurse had told her the day before. She remembered the conversation as though – well, almost as though it had occurred only the previous day.

She was still taking pills for her problem and they affected her memory sometimes. But she was quite definite in her mind. She was being released, correction - discharged, that day. Violet knew what that meant. She was no longer considered a danger to herself or the residents of Inverness.

In a way it was a pity she was being allowed home. She had quite enjoyed her stay in the mental hospital. The seven months had gone quickly and she would be home for Christmas, assuming of course that her mother let her back in the house. It had taken a few weeks to repair the fire damage to the house. She only set the bed clothes on fire because the police had called at the house to question her about the fire at the Kessock School. That really had been a good fire. She had heard that the school would not be rebuilt because of the extensive damage. The dreaded Kessock School was no more. She would go down in Ferry folk-lore.

The doctors had said that she was better. They suspected that there was some deep-rooted anxiety that was causing her to behave the way she did, some trauma in her past. Whatever the reason, Violet kept the secret to herself.

She had made a promise to them. No more lighting fires. She would be a good girl from now on. And perhaps when she got out she might be able to date John Urquhart. She had seen

Johnny at the school reunion but she had little chance to speak to him as the police had disrupted the evening.

She had a soft spot for John. She knew that he secretly fancied her. He always had done. She had only set fire to the old farmhouse because she wanted to see him. They were both eleven years of age at the time. John was in charge of the Cowboys who were hiding out in the farmhouse. She was a squaw in the Indian party attacking the Cowboys. Setting fire to the building seemed the easiest way to get them out. She had not understood why Johnny and the other children had run away from her. Nor why the police had been called.

Setting fire to the church hall a few years later had not been entirely her fault. She had simply asked if she could be a Sunday school teacher. They should have allowed her instead of saying that she was not suitable. After all, there was nothing in the Ten Commandments stating "thou shalt not start fires."

Doctor Jamieson was the one who had made the decision that she could be released. Oops! She had used that word again. She meant "discharged" of course. Doctor Jamieson was nice. He was not a real doctor. He did not fix bones or cut people up. He just spoke nicely to his patients. She fancied him even though he was older than her father. But there were few men that Violet did not fancy.

She missed her Dad. She recalled the time when the police had called at her home near the end of the war. How the police had said that her father was classified as a deserter as he had not returned to his unit following a brief leave at home. But Violet knew different. Violet had only been four at the time but she thought she knew precisely where her father was on the day the police had called.

The police had called her an arsonist after the Kessock School incident. She did not like that word. It made her sound like a criminal.

Violet thought of Billy Wilson. John had seen them together at the school reunion. She hoped that he had not got the wrong impression. Billy was not really her boy-friend. They did girl and boy things together but not "IT". She was saving herself for John. She only went with Billy because he was strong. He was the bouncer at the Caley Ballroom. Billy got quite upset when people gave her strange looks. But there was no need for John Urquhart to feel jealous. She would be John's girl one day. However long it took.

Doctor Jamieson held her hand as he spoke to her about her recovery. He reassured her that she was fully recovered. He meant, but did not say, "For the time being". He was in no doubt that Violet had serious mental problems.

She picked up her holdall and walked out of the small room that had been her home for seven months. She had not been outside the hospital in that time.

As she walked through the reception area she paused at the charity stall located just inside the main door. She was amazed at the amount of bric-a-brac donated by wellwishers in order to raise money for the welfare of the patients.

She picked up the Ronson Varaflame lighter. It felt smooth all over, a comfortable shape. Kind of sexy really. More of a man's lighter. It looked almost new. The price sticker said threepence, which was the exact amount of money she had been given by the hospital for her bus fare to the Ferry.

She looked out of the reception door and saw the bus pulling up.

She did not hesitate. She boarded the bus. She recognised the conductor even though she had not seen him since the Kessock school days. It would have been difficult not to recognise him. Donnie Burns wore a permanent eye-patch as the result of playing with live ammunition during the war. She handed her three-penny piece to Donnie, who turned pale when he saw her.

Snow was falling lightly as she looked out of the bus window and saw Inverness far below the heights of Craig Dunain.

She smiled a small smile.

She was grinning broadly as she stepped off the bus in the town centre. She would walk the rest of the way home. She wanted to do some window shopping.

One hand clutched her holdall as she gazed in the shop windows at the festive treats.

Her other hand was in her pocket. Fondling the lighter she had stolen from the charity stall.

It felt good to be back in action.

She was glad that she had a male doctor. Men were so gullible.

By the time she had reached her home in Kessock Avenue she was laughing out loud. At that moment, without doubt, Violet was the happiest madwoman in Scotland.

CHAPTER SIX

FEBRUARY 1963

INVERNESS

Police Constable David Thomson of the Highland Constabulary was on a high. He cycled along Academy Street heading for the Ferry district without a care in the world. Even the thought of his beat having been transferred from the sedate Crown district to the Ferry district did not perturb him. After seven years of obsession over minister's daughter Moira Ferguson she had finally agreed that she would go out with him. He was ten years older than Moira, but having just been promoted to Police Constable after thirteen years as a probationary officer, he felt that he was heading for better things.

His promotion had come about due to his diligence in the arrest of Marie Winngate. He was at a loss to understand why she had been released by the Chief Constable. The Chief Constable had stated that the release was on "grounds of National security." But that was clearly nonsense. He felt sure that there was more to the release than met the eye. He had been making discreet enquiries in the ten months since the incident but had found nothing of significance. But he would find out. He was ambitious.

He had a bit of a reputation as being a do-gooder whilst in the respected Crown primary school. He lost track of the number of times he had reported fellow pupils for misdeeds. The pupils at his old school had been saints compared to the crowd at the old Kessock School. He wished that he had gone to the Kessock instead. He would have had a great time reporting misdemeanours at the "Kessie".

Head in the clouds, he contemplated a future with Moira. Not that their discussions had got that far. After all, this was to be their first date. But it was Valentine's Day. There was a special dance being held at the Caley Ballroom. He had never been there, neither had Moira. His heart was beating fast at the thought.

It beat a great deal faster as the front wheel of his bicycle hit the line of bricks stretched across the road on the bridge leading into Grant Street. For once a member of the local constabulary had had his guard down as he entered the Ferry.

The cheers that greeted him as he picked himself off the ground startled him. He had not noticed the crowd of youngsters standing on the street corner.

He nervously looked around.

A movement in the window of a flat above the bookies shop caught his eye.

The noise from the street had brought Ally Henderson to the window. He looked out and found himself gazing into the eyes of a police constable. A police constable Ally had never seen before.

Ally reacted immediately.

He quickly removed two cases of Scotch from under the table in his combined kitchen living room.

Within four minutes the contents of twenty four bottles of whisky had been emptied down the kitchen sink

Ally waited for the inevitable knock on the door.

The plod of heavy footsteps could be heard on the stair landing. The footsteps stopped. The noise of the footsteps was replaced by a hammering on the door.

Nervously he walked towards the door. The empty bottles of Scotch lay on the floor by the sink. There was no time to dispose of them.

Opening the door slightly he peered out and was confronted by the face of Ronnie Jamieson, head of the local criminal fraternity, and Ally's boss.

"I've come for the whisky," growled Ronnie, breathing alcohol fumes over the white faced Ally.

Ronnie stepped into the room.

He stumbled as he stood on one of the empty spirit bottles.

Straightening himself up he looked at Ally.

Ally never saw the punch that hit him squarely on the face.

CHAPTER SEVEN

FEBRUARY 1963

INVERNESS

Billy Wilson adjusted his bow-tie as he stood at the entrance to the Caley Ballroom. He was expecting a busy but peaceful night. A normal evening would see a mad rush for the last waltz as the bar emptied and couples tried to pair off for the walk home. This more often than not ended in three or four of the lads chasing the same girl with the inevitable punch-up. However as there was a special Valentine's dance that evening the probability was that the couples who arrived together would be leaving together. Which was fine, provided the couples should have been together in the first place. It would not be the first time a slow foxtrot was interrupted with the words "Get your hands off my bloody wife" as an errant husband, out for the evening with his dolly-bird, bumped into his wife on the dance-floor - a wife who should have been at home looking after the kids. A wife who thought her husband was in Glasgow on business. But only because he had said he was going to be in Glasgow on business.

As Billy stood at the door he wondered about his girl-friend Violet MacDonald. She had seemed subdued when he had left for work that evening. On her release from hospital (Billy had no trouble with the word release), Violet's mother had made it quite clear that Violet was not welcome back in the family home. The council had warned Mrs. MacDonald that a repeat of the fire incident would result in them being moved out of their council house.

Violet moved in with Billy's family which displeased Billy's mother who was concerned about Violet being left in the house for long periods of time without proper supervision. This occurred when Mrs. Wilson was at work as a hostess at the

Harbour Inn and Billy was at the Caley Ballroom. This only left Billy's sister Mary in the house with Violet. Mary was about as reliable as Violet.

Mary had not worked for six years. She had been in a deep state of depression since she had been dumped by John Urquhart after an evening of dancing at Kiltarlity. Mary had told her mother and Billy that John "had tried to have his wicked way with her" before he had run away when her mother had arrived home from work. Her mother and Billy had accepted this version of events. The truth of the matter was that nothing had happened. John had escorted Mary home as she was too inebriated to see herself home. But Mary was desperate for a boy-friend and John was her knight in shining armour. And there wasn't too many of those in the area.........this being the Ferry. There was an abundance of frogs, but no princes.

Billy wondered which innocent girl was currently being seduced by John Urquhart's charms. He knew that the retrobate was still in the R.A.F. and was out in the Far East. Well, he had to return to Inverness one day. Billy would settle with him then.

Of more immediate concern was that he thought he had seen Violet with a lighter. The thought of a combination of Violet, a lighter, and gas, made Billy feel ill.

Billy brought himself back to reality. He had a job to do.

It was quite a surprise when Ally Henderson walked into the dance hall. The surprise was not that Ally was attending a Valentine's dance on his own. He was always on his own. It was because Ally was walking. Word had quickly gotten around that earlier in the day Ally had been given a good going over by Ronnie Jamieson.

It was to Ally's credit that he was walking. Judging by the black eye, bruising on his face, and a pronounced limp, he must have been in a great deal of pain. But Ally had not missed a Caley dance in five years. Ally had always stated that he preferred the Caley to the Meeting Rooms, the only other dance-hall in town. The truth was, every time he went to the Meeting Rooms he ended up in a fight, and was inevitably the loser.

But if Billy Wilson was surprised to see Ally walk into the Caley he was even more shocked to see Police Constable David Thomson with a very attractive woman on his arm. Local gossip had it that "Dopey" Thomson was "a bit of a fairy".

P.C. Thomson was excited on entering the Caley. He had every intention of making this a night to remember for Moira. Being ignorant on what to expect he mistook Billy for a cloakroom attendant and, taking his overcoat off, handed it to Billy and proceeded into the bar adjacent to the dance-floor. P.C. Thomson was really impressed. There were not many places where the cloakroom attendant wore a tuxedo. Billy was initially taken aback at being handed the coat but reacted swiftly by opening a window and throwing the coat into the car park.

The first person P.C. Thomson saw on entering the bar was Ally Henderson. The photographic memory that was installed in the constable's brain clicked into gear. He had seen that face before. Before it had been disfigured, that is. Recently! That day! Where?

The computer computed and realisation dawned on him. This was the face that he had seen in the window when he had come off his bicycle in Grant Street. Perhaps the man at the window might know some of the toe-rags who had placed the bricks in the road? He decided to speak to him.

Ally twitched as he saw David Thomson approach. He recognised the copper. It was bad enough getting a hiding from Ronnie Jamieson. But now the Old Bill had tracked him down.

P.C. Thomson only got as far as saying "I saw you in Grant Street ...." when Ally panicked and ran out of the bar, spilling his glass of Mackeson over Moira's dress as he passed her.

David and Moira stood there aghast.

It was Moira who broke the silence that followed.

"Well, I can't stay here all night in a wet dress," she calmly stated. "Why don't we go back to your place and I'll slip into something else"

His overcoat was not the only thing that P.C. Thomson lost that night. Moira made sure of that. The constable wasn't God's gift to women.

But no man in Inverness was.

CHAPTER EIGHT

FEBRUARY 1963

INVERNESS

Ronnie Jamieson stood up and closed the window of his office to keep out the smell of the gasworks and the nearby tannery. His place of work was a small house located in Madras Street in the heart of his Merkinch empire. The array of goods scattered throughout the house would have done credit to Aladdin's cave.

He tapped his pencil on the desk. His patience was nearing an end. He was rapidly coming to the conclusion that good staff were hard to come by. His run-in with Ally Henderson was almost the final straw.

He checked the message he had just received. A consignment of electrical goods was due from Glasgow within a few weeks. State of the art record players, gramophones and 12" black and white television sets. All he had to do was reassure his supplier that he had the resources to handle the goods.

At twenty-six years of age, Ferry born and bred, Ronnie was the local mastermind of an "import and export" business. He spent most of his time working in tandem with his father Eckie, who was the ringleader of a smuggling operation based in Aberdeen.

Ronnie's nick-name was Napoleon. A name he was proud of.

The name had been wished upon him when he was only twelve years of age. His mother had died suddenly and he and his sister had been sent to live with their grandparents on the Black Isle. His father was not there to look after them, something do with "being detained at Her Majesty's pleasure".

As Ronnie stood on the ferry boat Eilean Dubh he waved to

his mates on the shore. Standing there with tears in her eyes was eleven year old Loraine Dodds. Loraine was not only the school romantic, she was one of the few kids who actually listened to the teacher. As the ferry began its ten minute journey to the Black Isle she wiped her eyes.

"He's just like Napoleon going to Elba" she muttered.

Napoleon it was from that day on.

Only occasionally, and always behind his back, was it shortened to "Nappy".

Ronnie had been shocked when Ally explained why he had dumped the whisky. The thought of a large police presence in Grant Street was alarming. Ally had said that there had been about a dozen coppers led by a hard and mean looking sergeant. This description bore no resemblance to any of the local plod. He wondered if the local bobbies had caught on to his dealings and had brought in some real police from Glasgow.

He had one other thing on his mind. His youngest sister, nineteen year old Elsie, who worked in the MacEwans Arms in Grant Street, had been seen to enter Jocky Wingate's flat several times during the previous ten months. Ronnie had never heard the expression "don't shoot the messenger" and had promptly thumped the bearer of this news, a skinny spotty faced youth who was trying to suck up to Ronnie.

He decided to pay Jocky a visit.

If the story was true, Jocky owed him, big time.

And Ronnie needed a front man for the Glasgow job, a job which by all accounts was controlled by a very nasty piece of work. Ronnie had never met the gang-leader. He had no wish to if the stories he heard were to be believed.

CHAPTER NINE

OCTOBER 1963

SINGAPORE

Billy Wilson could have been no further from the truth when he theorised that John Urquhart was seducing an innocent girl with his charms. John's success with girls in the twenty three years of his existence could best be summed up in one word -zilch. This was only partly due to the period of time he had spent in the deserts of the Middle East.

John was no Romeo. He had never felt confident with girls. But these failings were an irrelevance now. John had found his dream girl in Susan Simpson. The fact that they were eight thousand miles apart did not diminish their feelings for each other. Testimony to this was the flow of mail between them.

In the eighteen months John and Sandy had been in Singapore they had thrown themselves into their duties. The work, involving the co-ordination of movements of troops and equipment by air to and within Borneo, was demanding but exciting.

The effort and new found enthusiasm they showed brought its rewards. A promotion to sergeant brought John increased responsibilities. In addition to working on troop movements by air he was also allocated responsibility for the movements of troops by ship. An additional responsibility was the booking of civilian staff attached to the Royal Air Force in the Far East who were returning to the United Kingdom by ship. This duty required John to make frequent visits to the main Singapore docks.

The new Sergeant Urquhart rose to the task. Nothing was too much trouble.

He quickly got to know some of the crew on the large liners which berthed in Singapore harbour. The liners were a far cry from the old Eilean Dubh ferry boat in Inverness. Most of the liners were as large as H.M.S. Eagle, the navy aircraft carrier he had boarded whilst on leave in Malta earlier in his R.A.F career. The comparison ended at size however. The liners were luxurious.

A chance comment from John regarding the luxury of the P & O liner S.S. Chusan brought forth an invite to tour the ship from a very proud purser. The ship had docked in Singapore twenty four hours earlier on a seventy two hour stop-over. The passengers were on a conducted tour of the island and were not due to re-embark for several hours. The purser decided that there was adequate time to show John the ship before the passengers returned.

Thirty minutes into the tour the purser proudly threw open the door to the main stateroom.

A large crystal chandelier hung from the centre of the main room. The furniture, paintings and objet d'art would not have looked out of place in a stately home.

Leading from the main stateroom was the bedroom.

The purser threw open the door to the bedroom. Speaking in a gushing voice, he commanded "Look at the ceiling in this room."

John glanced into the bedroom at the impressive mirror which dominated the ceiling. Seeing the semi - naked figures in the mirror John was immediately reminded of the works of Michelangelo in the Sistine Chapel in Rome. Not that he had ever been to Rome. His sparse knowledge of art had been gained at the age of ten, when along with half a dozen other goggle eyed scruffy kids, he had listened to a very emotional Loraine Dodds pontificating about the wonders of the world. Loraine had a captive audience as Tommy Brown, also aged ten and known locally as The Machete Kid, was standing guard in the doorway of the Anderson shelter with an axe in his hand. It was common knowledge that Tommy would do anything for Loraine.

It took John three seconds to realise the subtle difference between the Rome masterpiece and the one he had just seen.

It was the sudden movement of one of the figures that gave

the game away. A figure that was totally naked.

The movement and the scream from the king size bed located directly beneath the mirror directed the gaze of the purser into the room.

John was pushed back out of room as the purser backed into him.

The grovelling apology from the purser was deafened by a further scream from the bedroom.

The bedroom door closed.

But not before John had recognised one of the figures reflected in the mirror above the bed.

It was the eighteen year old pop-singer Billy Boston.

The purser was wringing his hands as they rushed from the stateroom area.

"I should have checked. I had assumed that Mr. Boston and his wife were on the island tour," the purser muttered to himself.

"His wife?" said John in surprise, having read about the partying antics of the pop-singer in the Ravers Review, antics that always seemed to involve several females, copious volumes of alcohol, and drugs.

"She must be something special for Billy Boston to agree to marry her. He can have any woman he wants."

"Yes" replied the purser, "it's all rather hush-hush. His wife is Felicity Fairfax, a very wealthy socialite. They both boarded the ship in New York. Three days after the ship left New York they asked the captain if he would marry them. Nobody has seen them since the marriage ceremony."

John could not wait to get back to Changi to tell Sandy about the incident.

But the news that Sandy had for John was even more exciting.

They were to return to the U.K. the following week. Sandy had been accepted for officer training. John was being posted to London Docks as part of an R.A.F. movement detachment. Their tour of duty in Singapore had come to an end.

After eighteen months separation John and Susan were to be re-united.

Back on the S.S. Chusan a very embarrassed purser was receiving the dressing-down of his life. In front of the ship's captain he apologised to Mr. and Mrs. Boston.

Mrs. Boston seemed nonplussed about the whole incident. Indeed she seemed more interested in the chap in the R.A.F. uniform who had been with the purser.

John may not have seen the new found love of Billy Boston's life. But Billy's amour had seen John.

Felicity Fairfax, aka Marie Winngate, could not believe it when she saw John Urquhart reflected in the mirror above her bed.

Eight thousand miles away from the Ferry!

In the stateroom of a luxury liner!

"Is nowhere safe from that moron?" she asked herself.

CHAPTER TEN

DECEMBER 1963

INVERNESS

Jocky Winngate was at his wits end. He was at the beck and call of Ronnie Jamieson. When Ronnie had called at Jocky's flat ten months earlier the demands had been spelled out for Jocky. The immediate priority being that Jocky had to stop seeing Ronnie's sister Elsie and never speak to her again. The next pressing urgency, and Ronnie explained that he would wait thirty seconds for an answer, was to either accept a good hiding or carry out some small tasks for Ronnie.

As far as Jocky was concerned there was no choice. The one thing he had going in his favour was his looks. Not that he was particularly impressive in that department. But whatever he had worked with women. Take that away and he was left with nothing.

A bitterly cold December night found Jocky standing in the saloon bar of the Kessock Inn waiting for his two sons Robbie Nelson and Terry Nelson. Jocky had called the brothers there for a discreet meeting to discuss business. The brothers still had no idea of the real relationship between Jocky and themselves. Jocky intended to keep it that way.

He recalled the moment of panic some months earlier when, in a drunken moment, Terry had put his arm around Jocky and stated that he wished Jocky was his Dad. It wasn't the comment that panicked Jocky. It was the arm around his neck. It was a sign of affection. Ferry men did not cuddle each other. The nearest a Ferry man got to physical contact with another male was a fist in the face.

Jocky lifted his head from his pint just in time to see

Robbie and Terry walk out of the ladies toilet.

"What the hell are you two playing at?" Jocky demanded.

"We thought you wanted us to enter the public bar so nobody would see us. We used our brains and went into the lounge bar, and then nipped through the ladies' toilet," replied Robbie.

Jocky glanced around the room. Every eye in the bar was staring at the shivering brothers as they huddled close to Jocky. The cuddle that Jocky had received from Terry many months before had not gone unnoticed. Terry and Robbie walking out of the ladies' toilet had simply added fuel to the speculation.

Had Jocky been a foot taller and five stone heavier he may well have returned the stares. As it was he lowered his head. He was in no mood to start any trouble with his fellow inebriates. Jocky was, after thirty years of philandering, beginning to realise that one or two of the Ferry men were beginning to question why their wives appeared to be so content with life.

Taking the risk of further gossip Jocky pulled his chair closer to the brothers.

"We have another job coming up, although I don't know why we are being asked to do the bloody thing. With the mess you two made of the last two jobs I'm surprised that we are still breathing."

"It was hardly our fault that the police were all over the Meeting Rooms when we delivered the dodgy spirits" stated Terry.

Jocky grabbed him by the throat.

"Did you not think that delivering the booze on the same evening as the Police Ball was a bit risky?"

Terry, trying desperately to breathe through the pressure on his larynx, eventually managed a few words.

"We reckoned that the police would be too busy that evening," he replied.

"So you parked the truck loaded with stolen drink outside the Meeting Rooms, right beside the sign that stated "No Parking. Reserved for Chief Constable" Jocky retorted, spluttering his drink as he did so.

Robbie interceded at this point.

"No harm done," he pointed out. "The police never realised

that it was us using the truck."

Jocky reflected on the comments from Nappy Jamieson after the failed drinks delivery. Nappy had come round to Jocky's flat to discuss the problem. Jocky had heeded Ronnie's advice ten months earlier that he should never see Elsie again. But by then the damage had been done. Elsie was already pregnant and had given birth to a son six months after the relationship had ended.

Ironically enough this was to be Jocky's life-line. Nappy was so delighted at being an uncle that he actually found himself liking Jocky.

But on this latest visit to the flat, Ronnie "Nappy" Jamieson had made it crystal clear to Jocky. Any more mistakes and the wrath of Glasgow would hit the Highlands. There was no more room for errors.

With a deep sigh Jocky outlined the next job to the attentive Robbie and Terry.

CHAPTER ELEVEN

APRIL 1964

INVERNESS

Mrs. Mary Wilson's role in life extended beyond being the mother to depressed daughter Mary and bouncer Billy. She was also the manager and mature hostess of the Harbour Inn. She was painting her nails when Terry Nelson walked into the bar. It was the middle of the afternoon and although the bar was closed to punters, Mary was in attendance awaiting a delivery. Her clientele were mainly foreign seamen from the many ships that docked in the harbour. But this suited Mary. It meant that the main business of the establishment, a hostess service for lonely sailors, was booming.

Mary had been under pressure for some time from the new owners of the inn to increase profits. Using whatever means necessary, legal or illegal. The only thing that Mary knew about the new owners was that they operated from Glasgow. Not that she cared who owned the inn. All she was interested in was the twenty pounds she was allowed to retain from the takings each week as her wages. In addition to this she made a few pounds as "an experienced hostess". She was allowed to keep all of this. The other girls had to pay half of their "hostess" earnings to the owners.

Terry looked around the bar apprehensively. On the only other occasion he had been in the pub he had been thrown out by Mary on the grounds that the police were looking for him and the last thing she needed was the unwelcome attention of the police. Which was rather ironic, considering the number of real villains she did allow in the pub. But she had the sense not to bar the others. Some of them were hard men. Terry however, well, all he needed was a good clip round the ear.

"I've come to see you about a drinks delivery," stated Terry stopping ten feet away from Mary. "I understand that you are looking for a new supplier."

"As it happens I'm just awaiting a delivery," stated Mary. "I have a delivery every week regular as clockwork. The deliveries are all arranged by the owners. I don't even have to sign for the delivery. I've had no problems so far so what gave you the idea that I needed a new supplier?"

Terry tapped his nose.

"Sources," he replied. "The same sources also tell me that your regular supplier will not be delivering today. Rumour has it that the van containing your delivery has," he paused for effect," well, let's just say that it got lost on the way here."

"Christ Almighty!" exploded Mary. "I'm right out of some spirits and cigarettes."

Terry grinned broadly. "In that case I may be able to help," he stated.

He walked across to the window overlooking the delivery area and rapped on the window.

Thirty seconds later his brother Robbie walked into the bar.

Forty five minutes later Mary had taken delivery of a consignment of alcohol and cigarettes which was identical to the order she had placed through the Glasgow contact telephone number.

Mary had no idea what the management normally paid for the drinks but the offer from Terry and Robbie at one tenth of the retail price was too good to be true. She saw the opportunity for the increase in profits that was being demanded. Fortunately she had not yet done the banking and was able to pay the sixty four pounds ten shillings in cash.

Terry and Robbie left the bar with the thanks of Mary ringing in their ears .

They had reached agreement with her that they would be her future supplier.

The brothers' boss "Mr. Big" would be pleased.

The Glasgow owners of the Harbour Inn would be pleased.

It was a win-win situation all round.

Or so Mary thought.

CHAPTER TWELVE

OCTOBER 1964

LONDON

The H.M. Customs and Excise launch passed under Tower Bridge on its way to Charing Cross Pier. The launch picked up the plain clothes policeman and proceeded to Hays Wharf. The crew had received word that there was contraband on board a freighter which had arrived from Rotterdam. The brief was to watch but take no action.

John Urquhart felt exhilarated as the breeze from the Thames blew against his face. He was in R.A.F. uniform. He was on the launch assisting the Customs and Excise who had been going through the formalities of checking a consignment of freight which had arrived at the docks from the Royal Air Force base in Ceylon.

The order to monitor the Algerian Queen made a refreshing change for John. Whilst he found life in London exciting he found his duties at the docks tedious.

But life on the river was different. He was so fascinated by the activity on the river that he had not even noticed the tall well-built bearded policeman board the launch and proceed straight to the pilot's cabin.

The hoot of a tug brought him back to reality.

The Algerian Queen was a rust-bucket. John estimated it to be of fifteen thousand tonnage and, judging by the activity on deck, had a crew of six.

The Customs officers went to work and discreetly spent ten minutes photographing the activities surrounding the freighter. They did not expect the suspicion of the freighter crew to be aroused. It was standard practice for Customs officers to be seen taking photographs and making notes on foreign vessels berthed in the Pool of London. But there was no indication of anything suspicious. The cargo that was unloaded would be checked against shipping manifests. The Customs officers were more interested in the cargo still on board. The cargo destined for Aberdeen.

A decision was taken. The freighter would be checked when the cargo was unloaded in Aberdeen. The local Customs and police would be notified.

When their work was complete the Customs launch dropped John off at Tower Bridge from where he made his way back to the R.A.F Movements Unit at Kidbrooke. The plain-clothes policeman stayed in the pilot's cabin until the launch returned to Charing Cross pier. From there he strolled the one hundred yards to New Scotland Yard.

CHAPTER THIRTEEN

OCTOBER 1964

INVERNESS

Chief Inspector Berk of the Highland Constabulary looked across the table at P.C. David Thomson. Sergeant Ian Saunders was standing directly behind the constable in an effort to read an article the constable was pointing to in the Daily Sketch.

"According to this he was found dead in bed," stated the sergeant. "There is no doubt about the cause of death, a combination of alcohol and drugs. Which considering his life style is hardly surprising. Although it does seem strange that he was smiling broadly at the time of death."

The Chief Inspector took the newspaper from Constable Thomson and glanced at the picture of the very dead Billy Boston.

He looked up at the constable.

"I'm not quite sure where you are coming from, constable," he said. "This death happened in San Francisco. We all know that everybody out there is some form of junkie. What has this to do with the Highland Constabulary?"

P.C. Thomson pointed to the other picture on the page.

"That's the Highland connection," he said.

The Chief Inspector and sergeant looked at the photograph of a very attractive young woman. The woman was dressed in black with a dark veil covering her face, clearly the widow in mourning.

"The former Felicity Fairfax, a wealthy socialite according to the report," remarked the sergeant with a quizzical look at P.C. Thomson.

"Don't you recognise her?" asked the constable.

The senior officers looked again at the photograph.

"Could it be Sophia Loren?" queried the sergeant.

As far as the Chief Inspector could see it could have been Quasimodo under the veil.

The C.I looked at his watch. He had a pressing meeting with the Chief Constable to report progress following the senior officers' briefing. Rumour on the street was that some of the pubs in the Merkinch area were being supplied with contraband booze and cigarettes. The odd thing was that nobody had reported the goods stolen in the first place. Which was strange. For insurance recovery purposes alone the thefts should have been reported.

"Get to the point, Thomson," the Chief Inspector barked.

"Don't you see," said an exasperated and excited Constable Thomson. "It's Marie Winngate."

The sergeant looked at the picture again. It was impossible to see through the dark veil worn by the widow.

But the sergeant recalled that David Thomson had a reputation for having a photographic memory.

"Was it possible?" the sergeant wondered. "Could the veiled widow really be Marie Winngate?"

The Chief Inspector was no longer looking at either the constable or the sergeant.

He was staring at the photograph in the newspaper with a glazed look on his face.

He recalled the encounter between Marie Winngate and the Chief Constable following her arrest in 1962.

He had deliberately erased the name Marie Winngate from his mind since then.

Hoping that he would never hear the name mentioned again.

He had a feeling that he would be in for a rough time if he mentioned the name Marie Winngate to the Chief Constable.

Best forget about her, he decided.

CHAPTER FOURTEEN

OCTOBER 1964

LONDON

Marie Winngate, the widow of the late Billy Boston, who by this time was pushing up daisies in San Francisco, was outraged. She had only been back in London two days, having spent the previous twelve months in the States, the first two months in her role as Felicity Fairfax, and the remainder of the period as Mrs. Bobby Boston.

It had been pure chance that she had been in the hotel lobby when Billy and his entourage had entered the hotel. She had recognised him straight away. There were few people in the world that would not have recognised Billy Boston.

It had taken a few discreetly passed dollars to the hotel concierge to establish which room Billy was occupying. The rest was easy. Whatever genes her father Jocky had were also rampant in Marie. Billy had stood no chance once Marie had put her mind to it.

The death of Billy the previous month had shocked the pop world. Marie had been less surprised. The way he had been knocking back the drugs and the booze she was amazed he had survived the wedding cruise on the Chusan. It had been hard work ensuring that he took the pills regularly during their ten month marriage.

What did surprise her however was the size of the estate she had inherited. She was a very wealthy widow.

Autumnal leaves were falling from the trees in nearby Green Park as Marie sipped her afternoon tea in her suite in the Ritz Hotel. Marie had walked through the park earlier in the day in an effort to control her anger.

The reason for Marie's anger was the information she had received from her team in Glasgow.

For the past seven months somebody had been hijacking the consignments of drinks and cigarettes that Marie's organisation had been delivering to their three outlets in Inverness. The goods had been stolen by Marie's organisation in the first place. It now appeared that somebody not only had the gall to steal the goods from her, but they had the bare-faced cheek to sell them back to her pub outlets.

Marie decided it was time to visit Inverness to find out what the hell was going on.

She just hoped that the gang who were hijacking the goods arriving by road had not got wind of the consignment arriving in Aberdeen by ship.

CHAPTER FIFTEEN

NOVEMBER 1964

INVERNESS

John Urquhart and Susan Simpson gazed out of the window of the train as it crawled through the Highlands towards Inverness. John had boarded the train in London and Susan had joined the train in Edinburgh. This was their first trip to their home-town in thirty months, since they had been re-united at the memorable school reunion.

Holding hands, John looked into Susan's eyes.

The question when it came surprised Susan even though she had been expecting it for some time.

"Will you marry me, Susan?" asked John dropping on one knee to the delight of an elderly matron sitting close to them, an elderly matron who had spoken non-stop, ever since she had joined the train at the same time as Susan.

"Of course I will, John. I've been waiting for that question for the best part of twenty years" Susan replied.

The elderly matron wiped a tear from her eye.

"Where do we intend spending the next three days?" asked Susan, aware that there was neither room at her parent's house or John's old home for them to be together. But even if there had been several spare bedrooms in her parent's house there would be no question of she and John sleeping under the same roof. Her parents were strict church-goers. The fact that she and John were now engaged would carry no weight.

"It looks as though we'll only have the daytime and evenings together," replied John wistfully.

Susan pulled him closer to her.

That evening they went to the Caley Ballroom. They

recognised a few old friends. But they were lost in the company of each other. They had no need for anybody else.

Walking Susan home that evening John was supremely content.

"One day," said Susan wistfully, "We'll be sitting in our own home with grandchildren."

The following morning John decided to explore his old childhood haunts. Susan was attending church with her parents. He had a few hours before he would see her again.

Midday found him in the harbour area. He passed the Harbour Inn and reflected on the terror the place used to invoke in him when he was a small child when he believed that pirates and vampires lived there.

He gazed at the two ships moored in the harbour.

One of them looked familiar.

It was the Algerian Queen - the rust-bucket he had last seen on the Thames under Customs and Excise surveillance.

He recalled the Customs officer stating that the destination of the ship was Aberdeen and that the Aberdeen police and Customs were on alert to monitor the unloading of the vessel and follow the goods to the final destination, believed to be somewhere in the Highlands.

He wondered why the ship was berthed in Inverness harbour.

Fifteen minutes later he was talking to Chief Inspector Berk.

Meanwhile in Ronnie Jamieson's pad in Madras Street a very concerned Ronnie was pacing up and down. As the room was only four paces by three paces there was not a great deal of pacing to be done.

Terry Nelson had told Ronnie that Mary Wilson wanted to see him that afternoon at the Harbour Inn. The request appeared to be more of an order.

Ronnie hoped that the meeting would not take too long. His father was arriving from Aberdeen later that day and he had said that he wanted to see Ronnie on an important matter. Ronnie could barely make out what his old man had said on the telephone. The old man had a tendency to hold the phone about a foot away from his face as though expecting to catch some disease. But Ronnie could swear that his father had said that the Queen was due in Inverness. Although why the old man was interested in the Queen was beyond Ronnie. As far as he knew his father was anti-royalist. Eckie had stated that he had another appointment in Inverness and he would contact Ronnie after that meeting had been held.

As though part of a concerted effort to add to the frivolities in Inverness on that particular Sunday afternoon, Violet Macdonald was on the loose. Violet had, on the spur of the moment, decided to meet Billy Wilson from work when he finished his stint at the Caley Ballroom the previous evening. She had been standing outside the Caley when John and Susan had left arm in arm. With the furtive cunning that only insane people can achieve, she stalked John when he walked Susan home.

She had been outside his house when he had gone for his morning stroll.

She had stood at the harbour wondering why he was so interested in one of the ships.

She was now standing outside the police station waiting for John.

She was pleased that John had not stayed at Susan Roberts' house the previous evening. She didn't really mind Susan. Well, she didn't hate her enough to burn her house down.

Fondling the lighter which she kept with her at all times, Violet waited patiently outside the nick. She sang to herself as she waited.

"London Bridge is burning down,
burning down, burning down,
London Bridge is burning down,
my fair lady"

This had always been Violet's favourite nursery rhyme. She changed the words because she liked the idea of a burning bridge. The other children used to run away in alarm when she sang the words with total passion in her voice.

As events were unfolding throughout the district, Jocky Winngate was under pressure. What should have been a normal Sunday consisting of a few illegal pints in the Kessock Inn at midday followed by an afternoon nap had been completely disrupted because of his presence being required at Jock's Kitchen to execute a repair on the steam vat used to make the tapioca pudding. He had been there for four hours before he found the cause of the breakdown. A hairnet was stuck in the discharge pipe. An urgent repair was necessary to ensure that there was no disruption to the Monday routine of preparing a whole week's supply of tapioca.

The repair had taken longer than he expected with the result that he found himself checking his watch frequently. He had an important meeting to attend.

At the Harbour Inn, Marie Winngate was receiving confirmation that Mrs. Mary Wilson had passed on her instructions. Mary confirmed that she had spoken to the two brothers who had been making the deliveries and they had promised Mary that they would be at the pub that afternoon. The brothers also confirmed that they had relayed the instructions to "Mr. Big". According to Terry Nelson, the mysterious "Mr. Big" had Glasgow connections.

Mary Wilson confirmed that the other person that Marie had wanted to meet would also be at the meeting.

It took John Urquhart three quarters of an hour to convince Chief Inspector Berk that the story concerning the Algerian Queen was true. A telephone call to London Customs and Excise was required before the senior officer had believed John. The Chief Inspector had not forgotten John's previous discussions with the police. A burnt out primary school was testimony to how dangerous Urquhart was. In no way could Violet MacDonald be held totally responsible for the incident.

The Chief Inspector set the wheels in motion. The harbour authorities confirmed that the captain of the Algerian Queen had requested that his cargo be unloaded as soon as possible which, as the dock labourers did not work on Sundays, would be first thing the following morning. A watchful eye would be kept on the freighter to ensure that no unloading took place before then.

John was advised that police would be on standby at the harbour from six o' clock the following morning. In view of the assistance he had already given to the police, his presence at the harbour would be welcomed.

John left the police station, heading for Susan's house.

Had he not been so preoccupied he would probably have heard a low voice singing:-

"London Bridge is burning down,
burning down,
burning down.............."

CHAPTER SIXTEEN

NOVEMBER 1964

INVERNESS

Marie Winngate stood in the doorway leading from the stockroom into the public bar of the Harbour Inn. She was strategically placed in order that she would not be seen by anybody entering the bar. She wanted the element of surprise on her side. Mary Wilson stood behind the bar. The main door from the street was locked. Only invited guests were expected through the side door.

Marie, wearing a long dark wig and sunglasses, held her breath to avoid inhaling the smell of cheap perfume, stale alcohol, and tobacco.

She had been in position fifteen minutes when the side door opened. Terry Nelson walked in followed by his brother Robbie.

Marie looked them over. She recognised the brothers from her early childhood. As she recalled, they were not exactly gifted in the brains department. There was no way that they could have masterminded the hijackings on their own initiative. Marie was intrigued. Who exactly was the mysterious "Mr. Big" and what was his Glasgow connection?

Mary Wilson gesticulated for the brothers to sit down. As she saw it, this was her golden moment. She had managed to secure a reliable very cost effective supplier and the woman in sunglasses from Glasgow, whoever she was, had made it clear that as a result of the meeting being held with the new suppliers there could well be some changes in the organisation. Mary had visions of taking over the running of the other Inverness pubs controlled by the organisation. Clearly the woman from Glasgow was some sort of mediator trying to broker a deal.

Two minutes after the brothers had entered the pub the side door opened again.

Ronnie Jamieson strutted into the bar.

The two brothers looked at Ronnie and nodded a greeting.

"O.K. Ronnie," said Terry.

Ronnie glared at the brothers.

Marie stepped from her hiding place and stood in front of the three men from the Ferry. They all looked at her, wondering who she was.

"Are you Mr. Big?" She directed the question at Ronnie.

Ronnie looked at her. "Christ," he thought, "this is some fancy piece."

"I have been called Mr. Big," he replied with a leer on his face.

"But he's....... " Robbie began to utter before closing his mouth as Marie gave him a look that would have terrified a Regimental Sergeant Major.

"So you're the one who had been masterminding all these robberies?" Marie said, looking Ronnie straight in the eye.

"Well, I will take some credit for it," replied Ronnie "although it's no thanks to these two cretins."

"Was the whole thing your idea?" Marie asked.

Ronnie attempted to look modest which resulted in a smirk breaking out on his face.

"I had some help in getting the goods," he replied, "but I used my own initiative in selling them on."

Marie looked at Ronnie.

"So you admit stealing the goods from me, and re-selling the goods back to me?" she asked.

Ronnie looked at her. It was slowly beginning to dawn on him that there was a problem.

"I'm not sure what you mean," he said apprehensively.

"What I mean is, the theft of my alcohol and cigarettes which you subsequently sold to her," Marie replied, pointing at Mary Wilson.

Ronnie was bemused. He had never dealt with Mary Wilson. In fact he had not spoken to her since she had made advances to him when he was only fourteen.

He looked at Terry and Robbie. The guilty look on their

faces was enough to convince him what had been going on.

Terry cringed as Ronnie advanced towards him.

Before Ronnie could express his feelings however, physically or verbally, the side door of the pub opened yet again and a figure walked in.

The smell of stale tapioca pudding wafted through the air, overpowering the other pub smells.

"Sorry I'm late," said Jocky Winngate, "I've had to work to-day."

"Thank Christ! You're here just in time, boss," exclaimed a relieved Terry Nelson who had realised that at any moment Ronnie was about to ask some question which he preferred not to answer. And once Ronnie was finished no doubt the Glasgow bird would also have a few questions.

Jocky looked at the brothers. It suddenly dawned on him that in addition to the Nelson brothers and Mary Wilson there were two other people in the bar. Ronnie Jamieson was there along with a woman wearing what appeared to be a wig and sunglasses.

"Sunglasses in Inverness in November," thought Jocky. "We've got a right one here."

Ronnie picked up on what Terry had said when Jocky had entered the bar.

"Boss. What the hell is this 'boss' business? There's only one boss in this outfit and that's me. And what is all this business about selling stolen goods to Mary Wilson?" Ronnie stated.

The brothers looked at Jocky.

Marie and Ronnie looked at Jocky.

"Are you the so-called Mr. Big?" asked the out of season sun-seeker Marie.

Jocky gulped.

Marie looked at the two brothers.

"You two can disappear," she said.

The two brothers fled. They knew there would be a come-back from Ronnie at some stage but they were prepared to put that off as long as possible.

"You," Marie stated, looking at Jocky, "go in the back room. Mary, you go with him and keep an eye on him".

Jocky looked at Marie. There was something familiar about her but he couldn't quite place it.

Marie looked at Ronnie.

"So you're Ronnie Jamieson," she said. "I've being looking forward to meeting you. I've heard all about you. We have business to discuss."

Marie pulled a bottle of whisky from behind the bar and placed two glasses on a table.

It took her ten minutes to outline to Ronnie the implications of the arrival of the Algerian Queen in Inverness.

She had no sooner finished advising him when there was a banging on the front door of the pub.

Ronnie slid across to the window and peered out.

"It's okay," he stated, "it's my father."

"Eckie?" asked Marie.

"Eckie and I go back a long way," stated Marie in response to Ronnie's puzzled expression.

Ronnie looked at her. She looked to be in her early twenties. How could she and his father go back a long way?

Eckie entered the bar and greeted Marie warmly.

"This is a bloody nuisance," he stated once he had a glass of whisky in his hand and Marie had updated him on her discussions with Ronnie. "As you know we were all geared to unload the ship in Aberdeen but word came out that the police were on to us. As far as the Customs are concerned we are due to berth in Aberdeen on Tuesday. It made sense to divert the ship to Inverness and get the freight off-loaded before the authorities catch on. The downside is that it means that the police now know that there is an Inverness connection. We had hoped that by unloading in Aberdeen they would concentrate their efforts in that area."

"I take it that the factory is all ready?" queried Mary.

"Fully operational," replied Eckie.

"Just think of the potential," mused Marie. "We could make a profit of fifty thousand pounds each year easily."

Fifteen minutes later the two men left the Harbour Inn.

Marie left the bar area and entered the parlour at the rear of the pub. She was thoughtful. There was a dark side to Eckie. She had heard stories of his early days during the war years when he lived in the Ferry. If there was any truth in the stories Eckie was not a man to cross.

Jocky was sitting at a table looking forlorn. An empty glass stood in front of him. He was wondering if he would ever have peace in his life again. Ronnie Jamieson was now aware of the private jobs he and the Nelson brothers had been running. There were bound to be repercussions from Ronnie. Now this mean looking bird from the Glasgow outfit was after his blood. How the hell was he supposed to know that the original supplier to The Harbour Inn was part of the criminal organisation that owned the inn. Things could not get blacker.

At that moment all Jocky wanted was for his life to go back thirty months, before he had got involved with Elsie Jamieson. If his daughters had not ended up in the police cells he would not have been sitting in the MacEwans Arms on that fateful day he had met Elsie. He would not have got involved with Ronnie.

Jocky held his head in his hands. "It's all that bloody Marie's fault," he muttered.

He was suddenly aware that he was no longer alone. Ten minutes earlier Mary Wilson had given up acting as his warden. She had retired to the snug bar and was half way through a bottle of gin as she contemplated her future. Even Mary could see that her stocking the bar with stolen goods, correction "stolen" stolen goods, had not been warmly received by the tart from Glasgow.

Jocky looked up at the figure sitting opposite him. She was no longer wearing her wig and sunglasses.

"I think that it's about time that you and I really had a talk, don't you, Dad?" stated Marie.

Jocky had been wrong when he had thought just a few seconds before that things could not get any blacker.

A wave of darkness settled over him.

Slowly, in a dead faint, he slid off the chair.

Marie instinctively rushed round the table to assist Jocky.

But the smell of tapioca was overpowering.

"Mary," she shouted, "where the hell are you?"

CHAPTER SEVENTEEN

NOVEMBER 1964

INVERNESS

John Urquhart and Susan Simpson were having afternoon tea in the Rendezvous Cafe overlooking the river as events unfolded at the Harbour Inn.

That evening they attended a carol service at the Empire Theatre. The Salvation Army were in fine voice.

The whole congregation put their hearts into their rendition of "Once in Royal David's City" - apart from one person sitting at the rear of the theatre two rows behind John and Susan.

The elderly lady sitting next to the young woman was sure she could hear the younger woman singing.

"London Bridge is burning down,
burning down,
burning down..............."

CHAPTER EIGHTEEN

NOVEMBER 1964

INVERNESS

A flurry of snow could be seen against the darkness at Inverness Harbour. It was seven o'clock in the morning and the combined police and Customs operation was in motion.

Sitting in a black-maria police van at the entrance to the harbour Chief Inspector Berk was running through the final briefing. Listening attentively were John Urquhart, Sergeant Ian Saunders, and P.C. David Thomson. A further four constables were in the Harbour Master's office located twenty yards from the police van.

"The unloading should commence at eight o'clock," stated the Chief Inspector. "Our brief is to let them complete unloading and then follow their vehicle. Customs have no idea what is being smuggled. The only information they have received is that the goods originated in Japan."

"Look," Sergeant Saunders whispered, pointing out of the rear window of the police van. "Isn't that Ronnie Jamieson entering the docks?"

An old beaten up war surplus lorry was making its way through the dock entrance.

"If I'm not mistaken that's the Nelson brothers with him," stated P.C. Thomson.

"I wonder who the fourth man is?" said Sergeant Saunders.

The Chief Inspector peered out of the window.

"Well, I'll be damned. I haven't seen him in years. That, my lads", the C.I. continued, "is Eckie Jamieson, a real villain. I thought that he was still inside for receiving stolen goods."

"Jamieson ?" said Sergeant Saunders. "Is he related to

Ronnie?"

"Father and son" replied the Chief Inspector.

Ronnie and his three companions were so intent on concentrating where they were heading that they failed to notice the police van. Their eyes were firmly focussed on The Algerian Queen.

Confidently Eckie boarded the freighter.

Two minutes later he appeared at the top of the gangway and gave a thumbs-up sign.

As Eckie stood there a klaxon sounded.

It was eight o'clock.

The harbour sprung into life.

Thirty minutes later the dockside crane had completed unloading ten large metal drums onto the lorry.

"Get ready to follow and let's just hope they are not going all the way to Aberdeen," said the Chief Inspector to P.C. Thomson who was in the driver's seat of the black- maria.

In the flat above the Harbour Inn, Marie Winngate was looking down on the docks. It was barely daylight and snow flurries added to the poor visibility. But she could see the unloading taking place. She could also see the police van. What Marie could not see was the bearded man with coat collar turned up gazing at her through binoculars. The man was smiling as he looked at Marie.

But even if Marie had seen the man she would not have recognised him. She had last seen him at the 1945 VE Day party down the Ferry.

Twenty yards away from the bearded stranger, Violet MacDonald was crouched behind a stack of pallets. She was freezing. The previous day she had overheard John Urquhart telling Susan Simpson about the police presence that would be at the harbour the following day. She had been at the harbour since six o'clock hoping to see John.

CHAPTER NINETEEN

NOVEMBER 1964

INVERNESS

The incident that created havoc in Inverness over the following few days occurred just as the final container was being placed on the lorry. Out of sight of the police a second unloading was taking place. This unloading was visible to Violet. She watched as several small hessian sacks were placed on the dockside prior to loading into a small white van.

Violet was not only cold. She was fed up. She knew that John was in the police van. She wanted him out of the police van.

Taking the lighter out of her pocket, the only thing of value she had in the world, Violet crept towards the hessian sacks on the quayside.

Removing an empty Malteser packet wrapper from her pocket she lit the paper and thrust it into the centre of one of the sacks. The task completed, she scurried back to her hiding place.

Whiffs of smoke began to emanate from the hessian. Within seconds the whiffs turned into clouds. Within ten seconds the sacks of hessian were alight.

It suddenly dawned on the driver of the small van that the goods he was loading were in flames.

The smoke from the hessian began to drift, fanned by the wind that was blowing the snow, which was now turning into a blizzard.

Ronnie Jamieson saw the smoke out of the corner of his eye. The smoke also drew his attention to the police van.

P.C. Thomson saw the smoke at the same time as Ronnie. Instinct took over.

Forgetting the reason for the surveillance he immediately

started the black-maria and headed towards the smoke.

The sight of a police van prompted Ronnie Jamieson into action. He instinctively did what all Ferry trained men did when a police presence was detected. He panicked.

With a screech of rubber the lorry accelerated. Due to the hasty departure however, there had been no time to secure the load or the tailboard. The unsecured containers started to roll about the lorry.

The container balanced precariously on the end of the lorry was hurtled to the ground as the lorry sped out of the docks.

The container burst open emitting a fine powder.

The smoke from the hessian bundles mingled with the powder and the falling snow and began to drift towards the town centre.

Chief Inspector Berk was pulling his hair out. He realised that if they did not keep the lorry in sight they would lose their quarry.

"Get on the radio and alert the station," he ordered P.C. Thomson. "Tell them to keep an eye on the Aberdeen road. The lorry must be tailed."

P.C. Thomson swung the police van round in pursuit of the lorry, and hit the white van side on. The police van and the white van both ground to a halt. Steam gushed from the radiator of the police van.

The smoke from the hessian bales and the powder from the container was carried along by the blizzard and fell as snow on the town.

Ten minutes after the lorry had left the dockside P.C. Thomson was trying in vain to start the police van.

Violet MacDonald was still standing on the quay. She had not moved from the spot she had been standing when she had seen the face of the man driving the lorry. It was the first time she had seen that face in over twenty years. The man had not changed his appearance in that time.

Violet shivered. Not through cold but through fear.

The snow continued to fall on Inverness.

CHAPTER TWENTY

NOVEMBER 1964

INVERNESS

The first indication that there was something strange happening on that particular Monday morning occurred thirty minutes after the sooty snow flakes descended on the town.

The Reverend James Stoddart was cycling from his church in the Crown area to the town centre and had just reached the top of Castle Street when he took it into his head that he could fly. Freewheeling, and with umbrella raised like a demented Mary Poppins, he sang at the top of his voice "Oh for the wings of a dove."

He came to an abrupt halt when his bicycle hit the front door of the bank in the High Street, narrowly missing the bank manager, who was standing outside the bank handing out five pound notes to passers-by.

The High Street was busy with office and shop workers heading for their places of employment. Rather unusual for Inverness, particularly on a bitterly cold Monday morning, was the bonhomie evident between the normally dour townsfolk as they struggled to begin another week. The fact that all three local football teams had been beaten on the previous Saturday would normally have been enough to ensure that there was a complete air of despair about the town. Not that the women-folk gave a damn about the football results, but their husbands were insufferable if their team lost.

This Monday was different, however. Cheerful greetings filled the air. There was an air of collective madness as citizens acted totally out of character.

At the Glebe Street Baths the Crown District senior citizens were having their usual Monday morning free swimming session. To cries of gay abandon, the normally sedate doyens of the town frolicked stark naked.

In a rare moment of affection the married women of the town suddenly found their husbands rejuvenated as conjugal rights were resumed. In more than one case however the passion ended abruptly when, in a moment of passion, the name "Jocky" was uttered by a forgetful wife.

The monthly meeting of the Town Planning Committee was in full swing when Councillor Dicky Ryan, the Leader of the Committee, raised both arms in the air and said that he had a vision of the town one day having city status with concrete office blocks and fast food outlets replacing some of the historic town centre buildings. He was good naturedly told to sit down with cries of "he's off his head".

Ten minutes later he stood up and stated that he was homosexual.

He was given three standing ovations by a clearly demented committee.

The Herald reporter covering the meeting scribbled furiously.

For seven days the sanest people in the town were the residents of the mental hospital.

One person unaffected by the air of joy sweeping the town was the editor of The Herald. Known as "Sniffler", because of his obvious sinus problems, Bill Damson produced a forty page newspaper that week, twenty pages more than normal. The report on the comments made by Councillor Ryan at the Planning Committee made front page headlines. Story after story appeared regarding strange occurrences in and around the town. The leader in the paper queried whether there was some type of poison gas in the air.

Bill Damson was nearly right.

The combination of the experimental powdered whisky smuggled in from Japan in the metal containers and the smoke from the cannabis plants in the hessian sacks may not have been a poisonous gas, but it was certainly mind blowing.

The citizens of the town licked the alcohol based narcotic

snow from their lips.

The swinging sixties arrived and departed Inverness in a seven day period in 1964.

CHAPTER TWENTY ONE

DECEMBER 1964

INVERNESS

Jocky Winngate raised the glass to his lips. He was sampling the first bottle of whisky to be produced at the secret distilling plant using the Japanese ingredients.

The Chief Inspector's fears that the lorry being driven by Ronnie Jamieson may have been heading for Aberdeen were unfounded. It had taken Ronnie only four minutes to reach the secret destination.

Only Marie Winngate would have had the gall to suggest that the old fire-damaged Kessock School be used for the distilling plant. The school was a burnt - out shell. But the janitor's house which stood in the school grounds was in a reasonable condition. The local council had erected hoarding to prevent trespassing on the property. But a mere physical barrier was no deterrent to Marie. With the track record of the council it was likely that the buildings would be left in a derelict condition for years before demolition. Appointing Jocky as the supremo of the illegal distilling operation and her public house activities in the town on a tax free income which was ten times higher than he was paid at Jock's Kitchen ensured Jocky's allegiance and loyalty to Marie. His role at Jock's Kitchen continued however. A degree of normality had to be maintained. Or as normal as any aspect of Ferry life appeared to the outside world.

The driver of the white van which had been sitting alongside the Algerian Queen was released once the police had established that the consignment of cannabis plants he had been collecting was a bona fide delivery to a botanical garden on the west coast of Scotland.

The police vehicle was a write off with damage estimated at two hundred pounds. There were no serious injuries, although Chief Inspector Berk's pride was severely dented. There were no charges levied. Without any evidence no crime had been committed.

The Highland Constabulary searched for the old lorry without success.

The only real casualty of the Algerian Queen incident was Violet MacDonald. Whoever she saw that day, and whatever incident in her past the person reminded her of, had affected her badly. She spoke only when spoken to and lost interest in everything, including John Urquhart and Billy Williams.

Whatever was disturbing Violet was her secret.

It was to be a further ten years before she revealed her secret.

CHAPTER TWENTY TWO

DECEMBER 1964

INVERNESS

The Christmas dance at the Royal Northern Infirmary Nurses' Home was in full swing when Leslie Graham entered the hall. Leslie was one of the few male nurses at the hospital. There was no shortage of male dance partners for the female nurses however. The young blades of the town flocked to a dance at the Nurses Home like bees round a honey-pot.

This was only the second time that Leslie had attended one of the dances at the hospital. Shortly after his arrival five years earlier he had taken his cousin Susan Simpson there. This time he was on his own.

Leslie was more of a man's man and whatever free time he had was spent in the company of his mates, in particular James Urquhart, the elder brother of John. Leslie had decided at the last minute to attend the dance. The choice was either sitting in his room at the Nurses' Home studying medicine or going to the dance. Curiosity won him over.

He cast his eye around the room. He recognised some of the nurses. He saw them most days.

Two hours later, with earlier inhibitions having been cast to the wind, Leslie was seated whilst trying to recover from an exhausting "Dashing White Sergeant ".

He felt rather than heard someone speaking to him and he looked up. He found himself gazing into a face that he had seen frequently whilst tending the wards. He had never actually spoken to the face before, just a brief nod between busy colleagues. He had only ever seen her on the wards, never in the Nurses' Home.

"I'll only ask you one more time," the face stated.

Leslie suddenly realised that it was a Ladies' Choice.

The sounds of a slow foxtrot started up and Leslie stepped on the floor with his admirer.

"I'm Alison, Alison Forbes," the face said, a face with the most beautiful pair of eyes that Leslie had ever seen.

One hour later Leslie was walking Alison home. She lived with her grandmother in a large house in the Hill District.

The couple held hands as they crossed the swing bridge over the River Ness.

CHAPTER TWENTY THREE

APRIL 1965

INVERNESS

Business was booming at the Inverness drinking establishments owned by Marie Winngate. She had added a further two acquisitions to her portfolio in the previous six months. Jocky was now the man behind the scenes, the supremo in charge of five drinking dens.

The rumours about cheap booze being served in some of the town pubs, particularly those in the Ferry and Merkinch areas, began to filter back to Chief Inspector Berk. A decision was made. Somebody would have to go undercover. The question was - who? All the police in town were known to the villains, although P.C. Thomson was still a relatively new face.

Which explains why, on a wet and windy April evening, P.C. Thomson entered the Harbour Inn in disguise. What appeared to be make-up on his face was smeared due to the rain and his false moustache was a bit obvious but that aside he was very much in disguise. The fez he wore on his head was clearly a Boys' Brigade pill box hat covered in velvet. Which would have been fine if the metallic numerals 1and 2 were not clearly visible on the front of the fez. The baggy trousers he wore fitted in with the image of a seaman from the Middle East as did the red waistcoat. His size ten police issue boots matched quite well with the rest of the outfit.

David Thomson stood at the bar. He had never been in a public house before. He was not quite sure of the protocol. He had not even had the opportunity to order a drink on the night he had taken Moira to the Caley dance.

Mrs. Mary Wilson approached him, wondering not so much

who he was, but what he was supposed to be. Why he was dressed as a Turk was beyond her comprehension. There were only two Scandinavian vessels berthed in the harbour. It was inconceivable that a Turk would be serving on one of those vessels.

"What would you like to drink?" was Mary's opening thrust.

The policeman hesitated. He had to keep all his faculties about him. He was on important undercover work.

He looked at the range of bottles behind the bar. He tried to think of a drink that he could safely have without it affecting him too much. He recalled what Moira had said she had wanted to drink when they had entered the Caley Ballroom.

"I'll have a Babycham please," he replied.

Mary Wilson looked at the odd individual standing in front of her.

"Oh my God," she thought "I've got a bloody nutter in the bar."

"I'm sorry," Mary replied, "we don't sell Babycham. Do you have any other preference?"

David Thomson looked at the bottles behind the bar. He was sweating. The result was an even more gruesome mixture of make-up running down his face. The fake tan he had applied was fading fast.

Mary looked at him. She was convinced that it was Oxo gravy running down his face.

"Oxo?" she muttered to herself.

David brightened. "That would be lovely," he said.

Mary looked at him. "What would be lovely?" she asked.

"A cup of Oxo," replied David.

That did it for Mary. She pulled herself up to her full height and smiled.

David reeled back, terrified. He had never seen anything more frightening.

"Listen, laddie," stated Mary, "this is a respectable pub for hard working people. We don't like poofs in here. Now make your mind up what drink you want or I'll throw you out."

P.C. Thomson looked at the bottles again. Whisky. Gin. Dark Rum.

"I'll have a whisky," he stated.

"Do you have a preference?" Mary asked.

The constable looked at the hand written sign on one of the whisky bottles. "Nippon Special Blend. Two Shillings."

"I'll have a glass of that please," he said, pointing to the Nippon Special.

Mary looked at him. He clearly had no idea what he was about to drink. The experimental Japanese stuff had already hospitalised three of her customers. But at two shillings for a double nip there was a great demand for the alcohol. In fact it looked as though she might have to double her order for the following week.

David Thomson picked up the amber looking liquid and glanced around the bar. Every eye in the bar was upon him. His eyes stopped swivelling as he caught sight of a face he recognised. Ally Henderson was sitting at a corner table in the company of a young woman who was clearly not his daughter. Or, if it was his daughter, what he was doing was socially unacceptable.

The constable quickly averted his gaze as Ally Henderson looked him straight in the face. He was so preoccupied that he had swallowed some of the whisky before he realised what he was doing

The fiery liquid caught in his throat and he found himself unable to breathe. He spluttered in an attempt to catch his breath. He had visions of never seeing Moira again.

Mary Wilson thrust a large glass of water in his hand.

"Here," she said, "drink this."

The constable gulped the water. His throat was on fire. The glass containing the whisky had fallen on the floor where it lay in smithereens.

A wave of sympathy hit Mary Wilson. She didn't particularly like nutters but this idiot was more to be pitied than feared.

She pulled up a chair for David.

"Are you okay, lad?" she asked.

David mumbled something which she took to be confirmation that he was okay.

"I suggest that you have something less strong," said Mary,

handing the constable a half pint glass of beer.

Mary looked at the strangely dressed man again. There was something vaguely familiar about him, something to do with the police. She recalled a rumour about one of the police being a transvestite.

Twenty minutes later, having drunk three half pints of beer, David had fully recovered his voice. One glass had been enough to achieve a state of drunkenness. The Japanese whisky had knocked all sense out of him. He listened again to the question the landlady had just put to him. A landlady who was getting more attractive by the minute.

"You don't happen to know anyone in the police force?" asked Mary Wilson.

David tapped his nose. "Secret," he mumbled. "Top secret! Undercover! Sschh!"

Ally Henderson was three feet away from Mary when this pronouncement was made. He looked at David. By this time the last trace of Oxo gravy had disappeared and P.C. David Thomson stood there, recognisable and ridiculous.

Ally motioned to Mary to join him at the end of the bar.

Twelve hours after he had entered the Harbour Inn, Police Constable David Thomson awoke to find himself laying in a strange bed. Beside him lay the young woman that he had seen with Ally Henderson the previous evening.

Head pounding, and feeling unwell, the constable crawled out of bed. He staggered over to the window, through which sunlight streamed.

Stark naked, apart from the fez on the top of his head, he peered out of the window. Looking down he saw a group of small schoolchildren dragging schoolbags along the ground heading for the Merkinch School. They were showing the same enthusiasm for education that generations of Ferry kids had shown before them.

One of the small boys looked up at the window just as the constable peered out.

With a scream the boy ran, swiftly followed by all the other children.

When the small boy related his story to his family, on

completion of school that day, a new dimension was added to the legend of the Harbour Inn. What could the boy possibly have seen standing in the window? His description of a white face streaked with a brown substance, with a strange object where his hair should have been, and the number twelve stamped on his forehead, brought gasps from his audience. When the boy further added that a young girl with no clothes on had put her arm around the thing at the window the locals were convinced that there was witchcraft afoot.

The police were duly advised.

Five days later Police Constable David Thomson completed his report on the illegal booze operation. He needed the five days to recover from the trauma. In his report he stated that despite spending several hours on undercover duty, there was no evidence to support the view that there was illegal drinks traffic. He could however strongly recommend sampling the Nippon Special Blend at two shillings a glass.

His report also stated that he had seen no signs of anything odd in the operation of the Harbour Inn and dismissed the incident of satanic rituals as absurd. "Who in their right mind," he stated in his report, "would walk about with the number 12 on their forehead, when it is common knowledge that the mark of the Devil is 666?"

His report was filed by Chief Inspector Berk. No further action was taken. As far as the Chief Inspector was concerned it was two incidents off the books.

The young boy who had reported the satanic sighting was dismissed as "another lout from the area".

CHAPTER TWENTY FOUR

JUNE 1965

INVERNESS

Two months after his undercover operation in the Harbour Inn, for which he received a commendation, Police Constable David Thomson and minister's daughter Moira Ferguson were married. Moira's father conducted the service at the church where she had been a Sunday-school teacher and the constable had been an over-age pupil.

Nine months later the couple became the proud parents of a baby son.

At the christening six weeks later baby Derek Sherlock Thomson wore a miniature policeman's uniform instead of traditional christening robes.

CHAPTER TWENTY FIVE

SEPTEMBER 1965

INVERNESS

It was a Sunday morning when the 20 watt light bulb that operated in Terry Nelson's head instead of a brain suddenly switched on. Terry and his brother Robbie were sitting in Charlie's Cafe at the Farraline Park bus depot when Terry snapped his fingers.

"It's staring us in the face," he exclaimed.

Robbie looked up from the cartoon section of The Sunday Post.

"What, apart from that bloody wall, is staring us in the face?" he asked

Terry pointed out of the cafe window.

"Our next business venture," he stated. "Our opportunity to succeed."

Robbie looked at Terry open-mouthed. What was all this nonsense about "business venture" and "opportunity"? This wasn't Ferry talk. This was "up the Hill" talk.

"What," Terry asked, "has Culloden Moor, Bannockburn, and The Ferry, got in common?"

Robbie, who was trying to figure out what Bannockburn was, thinking that it was some kind of biscuit, just stared.

"Battles!" exclaimed Terry.

"When did the Ferry have a battle? Apart from every Saturday night, that is?" questioned Robbie.

"The precise date doesn't matter at the moment," stated Terry. "What does matter is that the battle is going to be re-enacted next Sunday."

"What the hell are you on about?" queried Robbie.

"Remember our discussion last week. We agreed that we were not getting involved in any heavy criminal activities and we should break away from Ronnie Jamieson's organisation. Then I have the solution," Terry stated, pointing his finger out of the window. "What do you see out there?"

Robbie had no idea what he was expected to see, or say, but prompted by Terry's earlier comment replied, "our next business venture?"

"Exactly," said Terry, pointing to a single - decker MacBraynes omnibus. "That's our gold-mine."

Robbie looked at the bus. A group of tourists were boarding the bus. A sign at the front of the bus read "Culloden Moor tours. Every Sunday. Departs 10 a.m. and 2 p.m. Adults Ten shillings. Children Five shillings."

"Well, I see a bus. But I still don't understand," said Robbie.

"Let me fill you in," replied Terry.

Seven days later the Nelson brothers were once again in the Farraline Park bus-depot. On this occasion however both brothers were smartly dressed. They stood beside a MacBraynes double - decker bus. A sign in the bus window declared. "Battle of The Ferry Tours. See a live re-enactment of the famous battle in which valiant Highlanders protected their homeland. More action than Culloden Moor. Tours depart 10 a.m. and 2 p.m. Tickets Adults ten shillings. Children five shillings."

A group of tourists stood near the bus. There was a shuffling of feet as the tourists muttered to each other. They had arrived at Farraline Park with the firm intention of visiting Culloden Moor. The two nice gentlemen in the smart suits had advised them that Culloden Moor was closed for the day for refurbishment. Instead of Culloden the coach company had arranged an alternative tour.

"But I've never heard of The Battle of the Ferry," declared a strong American voice.

"It was all hushed up," stated Tommy. "The English took such a beating that they kept the whole thing quiet. The Highlanders were led by Bonnie Prince Charlie himself."

That statement seemed to clinch it for the assembled tourists. There was a mad scramble to board the bus.

"Please have your money ready," Terry called throughout the bus, "and don't forget the souvenirs at the battle site. Genuine signed photographs of Bonnie Prince Charlie. Only one pound each."

The passengers were all on board when it suddenly dawned on Robbie that he had no idea who was driving the bus. In fact he had no idea how they had acquired the bus.

"Donnie Burns," replied Terry in response to Robbie's enquiry about the driver.

Robbie stepped back.

"Donnie Burns?" he exclaimed. "You mean the Donnie Burns who is blind in one eye? The Donnie Burns who is a bus conductor?"

"Got it in one," replied Terry.

"Has he ever driven a bus before?" Robbie asked.

"No. But he's very keen to learn," replied Terry, "and he's doing it for nothing."

Just then Donnie Burns walked out of the drivers' rest-room. He was wearing a driver's jacket and hat. He was grinning from ear to ear.

"No problems getting the bus then, Donnie?" Terry asked.

"None at all," replied Donnie. "They laid on the bus for Culloden Moor but made it a double - decker as they were so busy last week. When Billy Rafferty turned up to drive I told him that the Culloden tour was cancelled. He's probably on his fourth pint in the Harbour Inn by now."

Terry looked at his watch. It was ten o'clock exactly. The thought of four pints of heavy beer by ten o'clock in the morning made him feel ill.

"Right then, let's be on our way," ordered Terry.

Ten minutes later the bus departed the depot. The delay occurred when Donnie experienced difficulty executing right turns because his driver's cap kept falling over his one good eye. The bus eventually had to reverse out of the depot.

The old horses belonging to the local dairy and coal haulier were standing in the battle area when the bus pulled up. The horses looked splendid with multi coloured crocheted blankets thrown over them. There was an absence of saddles and other tack that could be considered necessary by skilled horsemen. A piece of rope hung around the neck of each horse.

Twenty wooden clothes poles, each fifteen foot in length with a kitchen knife taped to the end, stood beside the metal dustbin lids painted yellow. Tins of paint stencilled with the words "Property of British Railways", lay alongside remnants of tartan. A dozen household axes lay on the ground.

At the entrance to the field of action a sign proclaimed "Toilet facilities at Clach park three-pence."

The battlefield was bordered by the Inverness to Dingwall railway line on one side, and the council houses of the Ferry on the other side.

Terry Nelson stood on an upturned Bon Accord soft drinks crate and addressed the excited tourists. Curious locals stood on the periphery of the action wondering what scam was being perpetrated.

Five minutes after Terry stood down from his podium the battle commenced.

On one side of the battlefield were the English tourists from the bus. There were eight men, six women and four children.

On the Highlanders side of the battlefield stood the balance of the bus party. Fourteen men, twelve women and six children of mixed race, all dressed in remnants of tartan. The double - decker bus had been full.

The English tourists were armed with the dustbin lids. The Highland tourists held the clothes pole lances and axes.

With a cry of "charge" the leader of the pseudo Highlanders rode his coal-horse towards the English. As one man the Highlanders charged. As one man the English tourists fled, pursued by half the locals from the Ferry, led by axe waving five year old Jimmie Brown, son of Tommy Brown the original Machete Kid.

The cheers from the large crowd of Ferry folk witnessing this organised fight drowned out the noise of the police cars as they swept onto the battleground.

Within seconds the crowd had dispersed. The Nelson brothers were last seen running along the railway track in the direction of Dingwall.

Two constables held Donnie Burns by the arms.

One of the constables read out the charges. One charge of stealing a bus. One charge of driving with no licence. Four charges of hitting stationary vehicles. One case of demolishing a bus-stop. Two charges of failing to stop when instructed to do so by the police.

Donnie Burns was fined a total of twenty four pounds.

Donnie kept quiet about Terry and Robbie's involvement. Donnie was grateful. He had achieved his ambition of driving a bus.

By the time Donnie's fines were paid Terry and Robbie were left with ten shillings each.

The description given by the tourists of the two smart business-men who had organised the tour had the police baffled. As far as they were aware nobody in the Ferry owned a suit with matching jacket and trousers.

But the Battle of the Ferry did not end on the battle-field.

Mr. Jeremy Hill, the London based chairman of an international property development company, who was on holiday in the Highlands with his family, had instructed his lawyer Mr. Lawrence Willoughby QC to take action against the Highland Tourist Board. He was not concerned about the loss of the one pound ten shillings he had paid for himself his wife and his two children, to view the Ferry battlefield. He was concerned about the loss of his thumb and two fingers on his right hand. He could not swear to it but he thought that his attacker was about three foot tall, had a manic grin, and was waving an axe in the air as he screamed obscenities about the English.

The Tourist Board contacted the police demanding that the perpetrator of the crime be found and punished. When asked if any child in the Ferry fitted the description "three foot tall with a manic grin" P.C. David Thomson replied, "Every bloody one of them".

The mention of an axe pointed the finger in the direction of Jimmie Brown. Two weeks after the battle six policeman and two police dogs were sent to collect Jimmie for interview. Three of the constables returned with Jimmie. Jimmie was in a straight jacket. The other three constables were admitted to the Royal Northern Infirmary for treatment for injuries.

When asked how many of the Ferry folk had helped resist

the arrest a very sheepish P.C. Thomson replied "None. But he did have an axe in each hand."

Ten policemen with riot shields returned to Jimmie's house the following day to recover the two police dogs that Jimmie had locked in the coal cellar.

CHAPTER TWENTY SIX

DECEMBER 1965

INVERNESS

The case against Jimmie Brown, a minor, was held in Inverness Sheriff Court one week before Christmas. The sheriff on this occasion was Mr. Alistair Horatio Farquharson, a sheriff not known for his sense of humour or fair play.

Appearing for the defence was Mr. Stuart Hutchinson, a well known local solicitor renowned for his ability to get any villain off the hook. Appearing for the prosecution at great cost was Mr. Lawrence Willoughby QC, who had arrived from London with an entourage of skilled advisers. Word had spread in the London business community of the disfigurement of Mr. Jeremy Hill. The English were out for revenge. The porridge swilling heathens had to be taught a lesson.

The public gallery was full. Such was the interest that Ferry folk mixed with Hill folk for the first time in history. The press box was full. The excitement was intense. It was like a Scotland v England football match without a ball.

Sitting on a pile of cushions in the area set aside for the accused was Jimmie Brown. Next to him sat his father Tommy. Jimmie looked as though butter wouldn't melt in his mouth. Father and son were guarded by six policemen. The pair had been thoroughly searched before entering the court.

Police Constable David Thomson was the first witness to appear for the prosecution. He outlined the events leading to the fracas in which Mr. Hill had lost most of his hand. He was followed by two other constables who gave their version of events.

For the defence Terry Nelson stated on the life of his grandmother, (who had actually passed away in 1946), that he had not seen Jimmie Brown in the Ferry district on the day of the battle. He was followed as a witness by his brother Robbie, who testified that Jimmie had been with him in the Hill district collecting money for the church benevolent fund. Three other reliable adult witnesses from the Ferry testified that Jimmie Burns was a credit to the youth of the day, which, on reflection, was no great reference as half the youths in the area were already on some form of youth probation.

Totally bemused by this time, Mr. Alastair Horatio Farquharson stated that a break would be taken for lunch and the case would resume an hour later.

Despite the solid and apparently honest evidence being given by the citizens of the Ferry in defence of Jimmie, Stuart Hutchinson, the defence solicitor, could see that if the prosecution re-called any of the defence witnesses the defence would fall apart. Mr. Willoughby QC had been making enquiries and had established that the solid reliable defence evidence had been bought at a cost of five pounds and a bottle of whisky per witness.

In the private back bar of the Gellions, one hundred yards from the courtroom, Stuart Hutchinson discussed the situation with the court officer Willie Stoddart.

"It looks grim, Willie," he stated. "I don't hold out much hope of us keeping wee Jimmie away from some form of institution, which will be bad enough. But the gloating of those bloody English will be just too much."

Willie nodded in agreement.

"Aye, it looks as though we'll have to change our strategy," he replied. "Leave it with me. I'll go back now to get the sheriff ready for the afternoon hearing."

CHAPTER TWENTY SEVEN

DECEMBER 1965

INVERNESS

In the Ferry district word was out that little Jimmie Brown was in serious trouble. A meeting of the residents was quickly convened. The assembled crowd soon turned into a revenging mob. As they marched from the same field on which the battle had been fought, they were joined by the business owners and residents of Grant Street. It was an historic moment. For the first time in living memory all the public houses in the Merkinch and Ferry areas were empty.

Led by Ally MacLeod, who was desperately trying to regain some credibility following the beating he had received from Eddie Jamieson two years before, the crowd made their way to the castle court room.

At the rear of the crowd Davie Thornton and Dickie MacRae hugged each other. Devotees of the dance art would have been impressed as the two men weaved their way towards the town centre doing a text book version of the Ferry Tango, the dance unique to Inverness. The necessary qualification for achieving a perfect tango was being paralytic with drink to the extent that you and your partner had to hold each other up whilst staggering home. It was rather like synchronised swimming without water.

CHAPTER TWENTY EIGHT

DECEMBER 1965

INVERNESS

In the court room there was speculation as to why there was a delay in recommencing proceedings. Thirty minutes had elapsed since the stated time of recommencement of the afternoon session. Whispered asides between members of the law fraternity, between the people in the public gallery, and between the press hacks who were sharpening their pencils, suggested that something sensational was about to happen. Had Mr. A.H. Farquharson been taken ill? Were there some developments behind the scenes?

When Mr. Farquharson resumed his commanding position in the court-room all became clear when Willie Stoddart stood to address the court.

"In view of unforeseen circumstances it has been decided that all questioning and evidence given this afternoon will be given in writing," Willie stated.

An hour later, an hour in which only half a dozen questions had been passed from the bench to Willie Stoddart and then to the witness in the box at the time, Mr. Jeremy Hill finally stood in the witness box.

The first ten minutes were taken in establishing his name and occupation. At the end of the ten minutes Mr. Hill was showing increased signs of frustration and belligerence.

The crux came when the sheriff passed a note to Willie Stoddart.

The note read - "I am concerned at the attitude of the present witness Mr. Hill. Is he dissatisfied with the way this trial is being conducted? Get him to explain his problem."

Willie replaced his handkerchief in his pocket, and passed the note he now held in his hand to a red-faced and angry Mr. Hill, who was calculating how long the case would be delayed due to this nonsense of everything being in writing. A Queen's Counsel and a bunch of followers-on did not come cheap.

Mr. Hill read the note that Willie had passed to him.

The note Willie passed to Mr. Hill read, "Please show the bench the injury you have sustained."

Mr. Hill looked at Alastair Horatio Farquharson, the dispenser of justice.

Mr. Hill stuck his disfigured hand in the air.

It was the first time in thirty years of presiding in a court of law that Sheriff A.H. Farquharson had ever had anybody in the witness box stick two fingers in the air at him.

The ill-temper that Mr.Farquharson was famous for surfaced. He valiantly fought to find his voice, which he had lost at lunch time shortly after Willie Stoddart had convinced him that a double shot of Nippon Special Blend would work wonders for the slight cold that he had. It was a bloody nuisance that he had lost his hearing aid during the lunch break. The damn thing was too cumbersome to wear all the time. He had just taken it off for a moment. Willie had helped him to look for it without success.

"Contempt of court," the sheriff squeaked, "contempt of court."

The public gallery erupted. The Ferry crowd cheered. The Hill folk hugged each other. The press box groaned as the hacks strained forward.

"Contempt of Court," Sheriff Farquharson called, pointing at the struggling Mr. Hill. "Take that man down."

Willie Stoddart and two of the policemen attending Jimmie Brown and his father, who had both been forgotten about by this stage, stepped forward to arrest Mr. Hill.

Pandemonium erupted as Mr. Hill beat back the attempts of the police to drag him away.

Above the bedlam the shrill voice of the sheriff could be heard.

"Case dismissed, case dismissed, accused to be set free."

Outside the court-room Chief Inspector Berk and a force of

thirty constables had been trying to restrain the mob for three hours. The police dogs had been withdrawn on the grounds that it was too dangerous for them. A telephone call requesting assistance from the local army barracks, brought the response that the Kent and Essex Regiment, who were temporarily based in the barracks, could not assist. The Queens Own Cameron Highlanders, the local regiment normally based at the barracks, were on manoeuvres at the time.

As the afternoon progressed the mob gradually dispersed. Word was leaking out from the court room that the tide was turning. Little Jimmie might yet be off the hook. The news was enough to sway most of the mob who were by this time having withdrawal symptoms. Efforts to find a public house open in the town centre were in vain. The proximity of the police station ensured that town centre licensing hours were enforced.

It was all a frightening new experience for Davie Thornton and Dickie MacRae. The four hours they had spent away from the MacEwans Arms had been the longest time they had been out of the pub in over twenty years.

When news finally emerged that Jimmie had got off and the pompous Englishman had been sent down, there were celebrations throughout the town. The celebrations did not extend, however, to Ferry folk mixing with Hill folk. Fighting the common enemy was one thing. But once the battle was over normal standards had to be restored.

At seven o'clock that evening a reconnaissance party from the Kent and Essex Regiment, in civilian clothes, was sent down from the army barracks. When the advance party confirmed that peace had been restored the camp gates were opened and the soldiers emerged. The Commanding Officer breathed a sigh of relief. His regiment had spent the previous three years in riot control in Aden, Cyprus and Malaysia. None of them had sufficient experience to deal with a mob from the Ferry. He had made the right decision. The safety of his troops came first.

The following day the office cleaner, whilst servicing Sheriff Farquharson's rest room, found a hearing aid in the waste-bin. He later handed it into the court officer's office, to the relief of Willie Stoddart who, only minutes before, had gone to the waste-bin to retrieve it from where he had hidden it.

CHAPTER TWENTY NINE

MARCH 1966

LONDON

Felicity Fairfax (aka Marie Winngate) adjusted her sunglasses as she strode through St. James's Park heading back to her suite at the Ritz Hotel. It being lunch-time the park was thronging with office workers laying on the grass or lounging in deck-chairs, as they listened to the band of the Royal Greenjackets in the band-stand.

Marie had just had a fruitful lunch with Jeffrey Streadman, property magnate and owner of one of the Derby favourites. She had bumped into Jeffrey whilst he was placing a large bet at Cheltenham the previous week. But not before she had listened carefully to the wager Jeffrey was placing. The odds of 10-1 against Jolly Rover were too good to miss. Her one hundred pounds win bet had brought her a cool one thousand pounds profit.

The sole objective of her being at Cheltenham had been to "bump into" Jeffrey. She had been following the latest gossip column news. He seemed a good catch. At eighty one years of age he met one of her criteria. Being a multi-millionaire and a racehorse owner also helped in the equation.

Marie made a decision. Jeffrey Streadman would be her next husband. It had been eighteen months since Billy Boston had died. A girl had to get over her grieving sometime.

But she had other matters on her mind. Earlier that day she had advised the Jamieson family in Inverness that she no longer wished to have any business dealings with them. There was something nasty about Eckie that she could not put her finger on. At some stage she would have to review her Highland business interests.

CHAPTER THIRTY

JUNE 1966

INVERNESS

Leslie Graham and Alison Forbes hit it off big time. It had been eighteen months since their stroll across the swing bridge leading from the Nurses' Home to the Hill District. They had been inseperable in that time. It hardly seemed possible to both of them that they had worked at the same hospital for so long without really noticing each other. There was a need for talk however. Leslie was leaving the hospital in the autumn to commence training at a medical college in London. His ambition to be a doctor was about to be taken one stage further.

It was with a little sadness therefore that they entered Alison's home. They had just enjoyed an evening of dancing in the Ness Islands at the end of what had been an exceptionally hot summer day.

Alison checked on her grandmother as soon as she entered the house. Her grandmother was in much better health. A great deal of her memory had returned and she no longer played with a bicycle lamp. Her illness had lasted twenty eight years, ever since her one and only visit to the Ferry district, when she had attended the birth of John Urquhart. As a direct result of that visit to the Ferry she had felt the need for a sweet sherry. She was arrested several hours later for being drunk in charge of a bicycle. She never recovered fully from the shock of being arrested.

Leslie picked up the copy of The Herald which was laying on the living room coffee-table. It took him all of five minutes to scan the headlines and replace the newspaper. He then picked up the photograph album which was on the coffee-table.

Alison entered from the kitchen with a tray of tea and biscuits. Placing these on the coffee-table she sat beside Leslie.

"Just family snaps," Alison commented, "mainly of my grandmother and me on holiday."

Leslie dropped the album onto the coffee-table. A loose photograph tumbled out of the album onto the floor.

Leslie picked it up and glanced at it.

He looked again.

Alison reached to take the snap from him, but Leslie held on to it.

The photograph was of a young man dressed in R.A.F. khaki desert gear.

"Who is this?" Leslie asked, looking at Alison.

"Just someone I used to know. Nobody important," replied Alison.

Leslie looked at the photograph again.

"Did he ever mean anything to you?" he asked.

"I hope this is not a touch of the green eyed monster," replied Alison.

"How in heavens name do you know Johnny Urquhart?" Leslie asked.

Alison looked at him, surprise on her face.

"He was an R.A.F. pen-friend of mine," she replied.

"He wouldn't happen to have been at an R.A.F. base in Libya?" queried Leslie with a grin on his face.

"As a matter of fact he was," replied Alison, "although according to him the base was in Russia, America, or where-ever else he could dream up. But how do you know John Urquhart?"

"It's a long story," replied Leslie.

Fifteen minutes later the story of how John's brother had connived with Leslie to write to John came out. Alison sat in disbelief. The thought of her Leslie writing pretending that he was a female nurse named Lesley shocked her.

For about three minutes.

By which time they were both reduced to tears of laughter.

Leslie's laughter increased when it suddenly dawned on him that they would be attending the wedding of his cousin Susan Simpson to John Urquhart the following month.

Leslie was dreading meeting John. He had not seen John

since he had treated John for injuries following the school riot and fire incident in 1962. It was only then that John had become aware that Lesley the girl was Leslie the boy. Susan Simpson was still not aware of the prank he had played on John.

Leslie explained to Alison that Susan's husband to be was John Urquhart.

"This wedding should be rather interesting," was Leslie's passing comment as he kissed Alison good-night.

CHAPTER THIRTY ONE

JUNE 1966

INVERNESS

The rare warm June evening was clearly having a hormonal effect elsewhere in Inverness. At the MacEwans Arms in Grant Street, Elsie Jamieson, youngest sister of Ronnie and mother of one of Jocky Winngate's brood, took it into her head that a life in Texas would be better than a life in the Highlands of Scotland. Accompanied by her three year old son she left Inverness with an American airman she had met at the Caley Ballroom only the evening before. The airman was on an exchange posting at the nearby R.A.F. base.

Eddie Jamieson was informed of Elsie's departure by a grovelling but rather foolish Ally Henderson who received a punch in the face for relaying the message. Eddie was still suffering from the hard time his father had given him because of the loss of the Marie Winngate business. Somebody had to suffer.

Losing all fond feelings of being an uncle, Eddie went round to Jocky Winngate's flat and gave Jocky the thumping he had wanted to give him four years earlier.

The honeymoon between Eddie and Jocky was well and truly over.

CHAPTER THIRTY TWO

JULY 1966

INVERNESS

The long hot summer was causing problems elsewhere. In the janitor's house of the old Kessock School what should have been a slow simmering cauldron of Japanese inspired alcohol was fermenting into a fast boiling cauldron of trouble as the heat rose to record heights.

Jocky Winngate had just left the janitor's house and was sitting in his newly acquired Vauxhall Victor when it dawned on him that he had left the windows of the still - room closed. The redundant janitor would no doubt have been surprised to hear his old kitchen referred to as a still - room but essentially that is what it now was. The car was part of Jocky's new image since he had become affluent following his assuming responsibility for the running of Marie's business interests in the town. For some time he had been considering moving from his tiny flat above the fish and chip shop in Grant Street. The visit of Eddie Jamieson the previous month had reinforced this view.

His new found wealth, albeit illegal, was giving Jocky ideas alien to the average resident of the Ferry area. He had made enquiries about a small house in the Hill district. He had the necessary eight hundred pounds in readies, and he was on his way to view the property.

Once the windows of the janitor's house were fully secured, Jocky took a final look around the still-room. The brew was simmering nicely.

Three hours later the roof of the janitor's house took off as the heat turned the lethal brew into an explosive mixture. Fire engines and police cars raced to the scene. It was a re-run of the

1962 school re-union incident. What had not been gutted then was now razed to the ground. The only evidence that there had been a house of any description on the site was a metal doorplate, badly damaged, but with the words "Janitor's House" just legible.

There was no indication of what had caused the explosion. Everything in the house had been reduced to ash.

In the absence of any obvious explanation a report was filed by the Fire Brigade stating that the probable cause of the explosion was vandalism by former pupils of the school.

Jocky was inspecting his prospective new home on the other side of town when he heard the explosion.

When he returned to his flat he discovered that several of his windows had been damaged by shock waves.

Jocky contacted his solicitor the following day. In truth Jocky, like the rest of the Ferry folk, did not have a solicitor capable of conducting a house purchase. Their normal remit was as a defence solicitor on any manner connected with criminal law.

Jocky persevered. Four weeks and three solicitors later he moved into his new home in the Hill district.

The women up the Hill were supposed to be different.

It would be a whole new challenge for him.

CHAPTER THIRTY THREE

JULY 1966

INVERNESS

John Urquhart looked at his bride as she stood beside him. On John's right hand side stood his best man Sandy Roberts. On Susan's left stood Jean Morgan, her chief bridesmaid. Following a ten day honeymoon in Jersey John and Susan, the new Mrs. Urquhart, were moving to London. They had acquired the lease on a two bedroom flat in the Beckenham area, ten miles from the centre of London.

John had completed his service with the Royal Air Force ten days earlier. He was back in civilian life. He was about to enter into a new work environment as Deputy Head of Security for an import and export company in London. His curriculum vitae had indicated his brief spell working alongside the police and customs in London docks whilst in the R.A.F. This had been enough to secure him the post. Susan had completed her university training and had secured a position with a law firm in Lincoln's Inn Fields, the area of London exclusive to the legal profession.

One hour after the marriage service John and Susan found themselves hosting their guests at a reception in the Nessview Hotel.

John glanced around the tables. His brother James and the rest of his family were there. Alex Todd, his friend from teen-age coffee-bar days, took great pleasure in claiming the five pounds that John owed him from a bet that five friends had made in their teenage years stating that whoever married first would pay five pounds to the other four.

Alex Todd was sitting next to Jessie Williams. Tommy

Ross was there. "Something to do with banking ", John recalled, although he personally would not have trusted "Tommy" with money. Tommy Ross had a heart of gold but a weakness for the good things in life. In this case the good things in life being alcohol and a flutter on the horses.

Tommy Burns, home on leave and in his army uniform, was sitting with Loraine Dodds. John was surprised to hear that Tommy and Loraine were married and already had three children.

Apologies had been received from Billy Saunders. Billy had left Inverness in his late teens.

"Still," John mused, "it saves me forking out another five pounds to-day." Billy Saunders had also been one of the signatories of the five pound bet on marriage.

His thoughts were distracted by Susan.

"Sorry, darling, I didn't catch that," John stated.

"I was just commenting on how well Sandy and Jean seem to be getting on," remarked Susan.

John looked at the couple. Sandy and Jean were in deep conversation. It was obvious from the look on their faces that it was not the state of the world they were discussing.

"I see that two people have not turned up," said John pointing to two empty chairs.

"It's my cousin Leslie and his girl-friend," replied Susan. "They said they would be late. Leslie had to attend an interview in London for a medical position. Their train is delayed."

"I'm looking forward to meeting them," stated John. "It will be nice to meet some more of your friends and relations."

Twenty minutes later John was standing talking to his brother James when he heard Susan's voice in his ear.

"There are two people here that I would like you to meet," Susan stated.

John turned round.

"This is my cousin Leslie Graham and his girl-friend Alison Forbes."

John stared at the couple. He watched as Leslie Graham, his one time pen-pal, was warmly embraced by his brother James. He watched as his wife Susan threw her arms around Alison Forbes, his one time girl-friend.

It took ten minutes and a stiff whisky before John had the complete picture and saw the humour in it all.

CHAPTER THIRTY FOUR

DECEMBER 1966

INVERNESS

It was the alibi that the Nelson brothers had tried to provide little Jimmie Brown with twelve months earlier that gave them the idea for their new scam. They probably would not have thought of it had the Salvation Army girl selling the Warcry not been waving a charity tin in their faces when she bravely entered the MacEwans Arms. She was only twenty one, from the Hill district, and rather naively got it into her head that all men on earth were equal - and decent.

Three minutes in the MacEwans Arms provided her with a swift induction into the real world.

It wasn't the leers from the men at the bar. They were just celebrating after a spectacular win by Clachnacuddin F.C.

It wasn't even the wolf whistles.

It was not even the dirty old man who sat on a bar stool. He just stared at her.

Even the one pound note that the old man put in her collection tin was no consolation for the apprehension she was now feeling. Had she known that it was the first time that Jocky Winngate had ever donated to charity she might have been a bit more impressed.

It was the way that the two younger men had been looking at the charity tin that bothered her. Their eyes had glazed over.

Had she known the Nelson brothers she would have realised that they were up to no good.

CHAPTER THIRTY FIVE

DECEMBER 1966

INVERNESS

Terry Nelson knocked on the front door of the large house. He had never been in Crown Drive before. He was mindful of the warning that all the Ferry kids received at birth. "Be careful of the people who live up the Hill. If you ever have to visit there take a witness."

Terry had a witness. His brother Robbie stood beside him.

They were dressed in Salvation Army uniforms which had been stolen from the local citadel the previous day. Which would have been fine if both uniforms were for male Salvation Army officers.

As it was Terry looked ridiculous in a skirt.

"Collecting for the Salvation Army madam," said Terry in a falsetto voice, rattling his collecting tin as he did so.

The lady of the house looked them over.

Terry rattled his tin again. A Cow and Gate dried milk tin which had been painted yellow with the British Railways paint which had been left over from the Battle of the Ferry scam.

On the tin were the words "Sally Ann Charity".

The lady of the house looked at them in disbelief.

She looked over her shoulder.

"Two potential customers for you," she called.

Terry looked at Robbie. "Customers?" he mouthed.

A tall figure hovered in the doorway.

Terry looked up.

Chief Inspector Berk's account of the incident the following day related how two respectable looking Salvation Army officers had called at his door with collecting tins. Before he had a chance to donate anything the officers had run away. He assumed that his wife, who was behaving very oddly, had upset the two officers.

By way of compensation he had sent a cheque for two pounds to the Salvation Army that morning, along with a note of apology for his wife's bad manners.

The scam lasted three hours. Terry and Robbie made a profit of three pounds fifteen shillings from their door to door collections.

On Christmas Eve the brothers paid the money into the Salvation Army citadel where a carol service was being conducted.

Guilt had overcome them.

They had recalled the hand down clothing they had received from the Salvation Army in their childhood, and the regular visits to the Salvation Army centre for hand-outs.

As Robbie said to Terry, "Even hardened criminals like us have hearts."

CHAPTER THIRTY SIX

JUNE 1969

INVERNESS

The wedding of John Urquhart and Susan Simpson three years earlier and their obvious happiness was the prompt for their closest friends to take the plunge.

Within two weeks of each other Sandy Roberts and Jean Morgan tied the knot and Leslie Graham and Alison Forbes became man and wife.

To complete the good news for that month Marie Winngate and Jeffrey Streadman were married in London.

CHAPTER THIRTY SEVEN

AUGUST 1969

INVERNESS

Jocky Winngate had no such ambitions of marital bliss. Jocky was by now firmly ensconced in his new home in the posh Hill district.

Jocky's earlier views that the women from up the Hill were different from those in the Ferry proved to be true. He had been in his new environment three years and not one of his neighbours had spoken to him. He put this down to snobbishness.

This was only partly true. Certainly if his neighbours knew that he was from the Ferry he would have been ostracised. As it was they could not quite make out who Jocky was, or what he did for a living. He was clearly a man of some means with his flashy new car each year, and the constant stream of young girls who were regular visitors to his house.

He had been seen leaving his house at six o'clock in the morning on a regular basis, dressed in what appeared to be overalls. Concern was expressed by some of the neighbours at the thought that somebody in a menial occupation was living in the district.

The change in Jocky's fortunes came about purely by chance. Jocky was in the Kingsmills newsagents buying his Sporting Life when he overheard two elderly matrons discussing recipes. Each matron had a different view as to the ingredients in bolognese sauce.

Fortunately for Jocky it was a Saturday morning and he was impeccably dressed in slacks and a sweater similar to one that he had seen Val Doonican wear on television the previous week.

Whether it was the sweater and the thought of Val Doonican that swayed the ladies Jocky will never know. But when he interrupted their dialogue to point out what the correct ingredients were they suddenly showed a great deal of interest in him.

Jocky tactfully explained to the ladies (as tactfully as a Grant Street man could) that he was head chef and director of Jock's Kitchen. Fortunately for him the ladies had never heard of Jock's Kitchen. Their children and grandchildren went to boarding schools.

The younger of the two matrons, who was sixtyish with blue rinsed hair, suddenly realised that Jocky was the new (three year new that is) owner of the house two doors along from her, the house where all the young girls entered - and eventually left.

By this time Jocky was in full flow about catering techniques.

He failed to notice the gleam in the eyes of the women.

Before he realised what he was committing himself to, Jocky found himself agreeing to give a lecture on catering to the Crown and Hill District Womens Institute.

His neighbour could hardly wait to get home to advise her fellow members of her coup. An experienced, intelligent, and definitely rather sexy gentleman would be addressing them the following Wednesday.

The following four days sped past for Jocky. So preoccupied was he in running Jock's Kitchen and Marie's pubs that it was with some concern that he suddenly realised that it was Wednesday evening and he was due to give a talk to a number of elderly women. The thought of a pint at the MacEwans Arms appealed to him more. Following Elsie Jamieson's departure to the States it was now safe for him to use the pub again, particularly as Eddie Jamieson had already punished him.

With no time for a bath or a proper scrub Jocky changed from his overalls into blazer and slacks. A pair of loafers with an open necked shirt and cravat formed only part of the sartorial picture. The Royal Air Force Fighter Command badge on his blazer pocket enhanced his appearance even further. Jocky had purchased the badge from a war surplus shop in the town market. The closest he had ever been to a military establishment was when he had been invited into the British Legion Club for a pint shortly after the war. He wore an air of elegance and respectability that would have done justice to the Culcabock Golf Club.

Jocky stepped out of his house into the warm summer evening. It was a short walk to the Kingsmills Hotel where the ladies held their meetings.

CHAPTER THIRTY EIGHT

AUGUST 1969

INVERNESS

Mr. Jeremy Everest, the Conservative Member of Parliament for the Highlands and Islands, was having a bad day. He had spent the afternoon holding surgery in the Ferry district of Inverness. He desperately needed a drink in the company of civilised people.

The surgery had not gone as planned. Instead of the half dozen constituents he had expected to see at the meeting, with the usual complaints about housing conditions and lack of employment in the area, he had been confronted by a queue of people with various medical complaints. No amount of effort on his part could convince them that he was not a doctor. In the end he had given in and had met their demands for medicine prescriptions and sick notes. What the local chemist and employers would make of a scribbled note on a scrap of paper he had no idea. Nor did he particularly care.

It was all the fault of that stupid personal assistant that had been foisted on him by Central Office. Why the idiot insisted on calling a meeting "a surgery" was beyond him. No doubt it was some daft English idea.

He knew just the place for a quiet drink. A large malt whisky would ease his tension.

CHAPTER THIRTY NINE

AUGUST 1969

INVERNESS

Jocky Winngate stepped into the reception area of the Kingsmills Hotel. It was his first visit to the hotel. The hotel catered for professional people. He was probably the first ever school meals cooking supervisor to enter the premises.

The receptionist listened attentively as Jocky explained why he was there. Her fixed smile broke for just a second as she looked at Jocky. He was rough - the clothes did not fool her. But he had an air about him. He was sexy.

There was also a strange but manly smell about him, an exotic smell of spices.

Jocky entered the meeting room. He was by now deeply regretting his offer to give a talk. What he knew about catering could be written on the back of a match-box, a small match-box at that, not the large Swan Vestas type. It was pure chance that he knew that the two women had been wrong when they were discussing recipe ingredients. He had seen the very recipe in the Sunday Post the previous week. It had only caught his eye because it was sandwiched between the racing results and the football scores.

With a sigh he glanced at the assembled group.

He looked again.

Jocky had not realised that the Womens Institute was open to women of all ages. There were some good - looking women there.

The evening may not be a total failure after all.

Jocky had been talking about food for fifteen minutes, without making any sense, when the telephone in the meeting room rang. It was answered by the blue haired lady whom Jocky had spoken to several days earlier.

"It's for you," she exclaimed, looking at Jocky.

Jocky looked at her. Who knew he was there? He hoped it wasn't that dozy cow Mary Wilson with one of her problems. That woman had eyes in the back of her head. She always seemed to be aware of his movements.

"You can't move in this bloody town," Jocky muttered to himself as he walked to the telephone.

He picked up the receiver.

"Yes?" he shouted down the telephone.

"Meet me in ten minutes at the Glendale Bar," a young seductive female voice commanded before the crackling line went dead.

Jocky put down the telephone. He walked to the rostrum. Every eye in the room was on him. Every eye was glazed with lust. There was sufficient power from the stares to power a small town.

"Any questions? No? Good!" said Jocky, picking up his blazer and walking out of the room.

The Hill district was still relatively new to Jocky and his first problem was to find the Glendale Bar. A request for directions was answered by a pointed finger and a glance down her nose from a bespectacled lady of advanced years. She was not fooled by Jocky's appearance. She knew a tradesman when she saw one.

Jocky walked in the vague direction she had indicated.

The sign read "The Glendale Hotel". A long driveway bordered by rhododendron fronted the hotel. It was quite the most impressive building that Jocky had ever seen. Whoever he was meeting had class. It was a million miles away from the MacEwans Arms.

The sign at the side of the hotel stated "Bar Entrance".

Jocky entered.

He saw her as soon as he entered the bar.

It wasn't difficult. She was the only person in the room.

112

She was slightly older that he expected. But she was a stunning looking woman. She clearly had taste and money, judging by her clothing.

She was sitting on a bar-stool with what appeared to be a gin and tonic in her hand. By the look of her it had not been her first.

"Hi," Jocky said nonchalantly. "I believe you want me."

The woman looked him up and down. She liked what she saw.

"Well, you don't hang about do you?" she replied. "And you must be a mind-reader. I could do with a good man."

Jocky sat on the stool next to her. Close up she was even older than at first glance.

"I'm Jocky. What's your name?"

"Rosaline," she replied, "and mine's a large G and T."

Fifteen minutes later Jocky had the full picture. Rosaline was lonely. Her husband worked all hours. He didn't love her. He showed no sign of affection. Jocky was the answer to her prayers.

Jocky thought for a moment. Apart from the bit about the husband working hard it could have been any woman from the Ferry speaking.

But this one had class.

It took a further five minutes for Jocky to be completely relaxed about the situation. By this time Rosaline had removed her jacket, had undone the top two buttons on her blouse, and had managed to raise the hem of her skirt by eight inches. Jocky sat there with his blazer off, tie undone, and the air of a man about to pounce.

Until Rosaline fell off her stool.

Drunk to the world.

They stood there. Jocky was holding her up. She had her arms around him, with her lips searching for his lips.

It was the Up The Hill version of The Ferry Tango.

The first thing Jeremy Everest M.P. saw when he entered the bar was a man's blazer complete with a Royal Air Force Fighter Command badge, on the floor with a ladies pink jacket on top of it.

The next thing he saw was the face of Jocky Winngate

staring at him from behind his wife's head.

"Rosaline darling, what are you doing?" he whispered in disbelief.

Jocky recognised the Member of Parliament from a poster he had seen in the window of the Grant Street Post Office. Something about a surgery.

Jocky immediately dropped everything, including Rosaline, and started rearranging his clothing.

Jeremy Everest just stared.

In thirty years of marriage he had never seen his wife with another man.

Meanwhile one hundred yards down the road, in the Glen Ale Bar, the young receptionist from the Kingsmills Hotel was on her fourth port and lemon. It had taken all her courage to phone Mr. Winngate and interrupt his lecture. But she would wait for another hour. He looked worth waiting for.

CHAPTER FORTY

JANUARY 1972

INVERNESS

It was an eventful month in Inverness. Devotees of the Births section of the Hatches, Matches and Dispatches column in The Herald learned that former residents of the town had been active, if not in that month then certainly nine months before.

Jean Morgan gave birth to a daughter to the delight of her husband Sandy Roberts.

Alison Forbes outdid Jean by producing twin daughters to the astonishment of her husband Leslie Graham.

Susan Roberts produced a son for John Urquhart.

It was not all good news. The Daily Mail reported the death of property magnate Jeffrey Streadman in a boating accident whilst on a holiday in the Philippines with his wife Marie.

Constable David Thomson, to the annoyance of his wife who was saving the free shampoo coupons on the reverse of the article, cut out the news item, and placed it with the other paperwork in the file he maintained bearing the title "Marie Winngate - Suspicious Deaths".

He would discuss it later with Chief Inspector Berk.

CHAPTER FORTY ONE

MARCH 1972

INVERNESS

An article in The Licensed Victualler advised that there was a change of management in the Inverness public houses owned by Glasgow based consortium Cheaperbooze. Mrs. Mary Wilson had been promoted to area manager, but she would continue to have responsibility for the day to day management of the Harbour Inn.

On the face of it the change was just part of a routine management restructure. What the trade newspaper was not aware of was that the previous area manager of the public houses had left the area at very short notice.

But of course nobody in the licensed trade, apart from Marie Winngate and Mrs. Mary Wilson, knew that Jocky Winngate had been the front man for Marie's illegal activities in the town.

The first indication that the staff of Jock's Kitchen had that Jocky was no longer working there was when they turned up for work and found the premises locked.

The news that there would be no school dinners for several days was greeted with joy throughout the town by all the school pupils.

CHAPTER FORTY TWO

MARCH 1972

INVERNESS

The pressure became too much for Jocky. Three years after his unfortunate encounter with Mrs. Rosaline Everest he had been hounded out of town. Not by a Member of Parliament husband on a quest for vengeance. For the twelve months following their meeting in the Glendale Hotel, Jocky had been stalked by Rosaline. Everywhere he went she followed. The fact that he worked at Jock's Kitchen did not deter her. With cunning peculiar to women, she had also discovered that Jocky was moon-lighting as area manager of several public houses.

For twelve months Jocky walked everywhere with one eye over his shoulder.

In the end it all became too much for him.

There was only one way out of the dilemma.

Marriage.

Which was why Jocky found himself taking a more serious interest in the female company he kept. If he was going to marry, it had to be worth his while.

Which explains why, at the age of fifty five, he proposed marriage to Evelyn Russell after an evening at the Culcabock Lounge Bar.

Evelyn Russell, spinster of the parish, but at the age of thirty six no maiden. Daughter of Charlie Russell, a business entrepreneur, and an even bigger villain than Eckie Jamieson.

Evelyn Russell. Known to all in the Culcabock Lounge Bar as The Martini Girl, because of her reputation of being available "anytime, anyplace, anywhere."

Rosaline Everest was distraught when she read the marriage

announcement in the Herald.

But Jocky's ruse worked. Rosaline stopped stalking him.

And life with Evelyn had perks. Within three months of their marriage Jocky was invited to join the Freemasons. There was no question of him being a suitable candidate. On his own he would never have been allowed near a Masonic lodge. Charlie Russell was the instigator. Charlie was the Grand Master of his lodge. Charlie had no difficulty in his proposal to have Jocky enter the lodge. Every member of the lodge had business connections with Charlie. There was no fear of Jocky being black-balled. Had Charlie sponsored the Devil he would have been accepted as a member.

The initial attraction of life in the fast lane with the friends of Charlie (all male) and Evelyn (all male) soon wore thin. Jocky was a down to earth man. He was not pretentious. He was more at home with a few of the Harbour Inn girls than the ladies at the Masonic dinners.

But the marriage seemed to settle Evelyn down. Jocky was finding it increasingly difficult to justify his evenings out. He had no wish to advise Evelyn about his involvement in Marie's businesses. Not once did she question where his constant source of money came from. She had once made the mistake of asking her father how he earned his money. It was not a mistake she was about to repeat to her husband..

Evelyn mentioned the word "children" only once.

Once was enough for Jocky.

He needed a change of life-style.

But where was he to go?

Not back to his old roots in the Ferry.

Not to Glasgow.

London looked good.

He telephoned Marie and advised her that he was leaving Inverness. He explained that he could no longer manage her business interests in the town. To his surprise Marie suggested that he move to London to assist in the running of one of her clubs.

The following day he boarded the train south.

Evelyn missed him at first.

But when she found out that she was pregnant she quickly

forgot him.

Evelyn may have forgotten Jocky.

But Charlie Russell did not.

Charlie was humiliated when word spread through his business circle that his daughter had been dumped. Not just dumped by anybody. Word had finally got through to the masonic circle that Jocky Winngate was actually a supervisor at a kitchen preparing school meals. That in itself was bad enough. But when it emerged that Jocky was also from the Grant Street area, and he had some dealings with shady public houses, the enemies of Charlie, and there was a lot of them, gloated.

Charlie Russell was not a forgiving man.

CHAPTER FORTY THREE

JULY 1973

LONDON

If Jocky Winngate had expected that working in one of Marie's clubs in London would be a piece of cake, he was sadly mistaken.

The one bedroom flat that Marie had provided for him in north London was small and noisy. When he eventually got to bed, which was usually about three o'clock in the morning because of the opening hours of the club, he was kept awake all night by the traffic on Cricklewood Broadway.

He had been at the Stardust Club for fifteen months in the position of deputy manager when matters finally reached a head. Following endless complaints from the girls in the club at Jocky's ceaseless attempts to get friendly, the general manager had to intervene. Jocky was taken off management duties. Whatever charisma he had with the opposite sex in Inverness obviously cut no ice with the strippers of London.

A telephone call from Jocky to Marie did not help matters. She made it quite clear that her manager ran the club and she would not interfere.

At fifty five years of age, five foot two inches in height, and nine stone in weight, Jocky was not the ideal candidate as a doorman bouncer in a West End night club, which was the role he now found himself in.

He expected grief when he first spotted the three men staggering along Waldorf Street towards the club. He prepared himself to refuse admission. He prepared himself for the punch that would inevitably follow.

Jocky held his hand up as though he was a traffic

policeman.

"Sorry gentlemen. I'm afraid that the club is full to-night," he stated, looking anxiously at the three men, wondering what their reaction would be.

The smallest of the three, a tubby chap with glasses, who appeared to be drunker than the other two, looked at Jocky.

Jocky stared back. He didn't want any trouble, but the four-eyed git looked daft enough to start trouble. Jocky got ready to press the panic button.

"Jocky?"

Jocky looked at the bespectacled drunken man.

"Jocky Winngate? What the hell are you doing here? The last time I saw you was in Inverness," the man stated.

Jocky looked. He did not recognise the man.

"The Ferry, Marie and Alison," slurred the drunken voice.

Jocky looked again. By now there was several other punters waiting to get into the club.

"I'll catch you later on," Jocky said, as John Urquhart walked into the club.

Two hours later Jocky was on a break. He was curious. He wanted to have a talk with John Urquhart. The last time Jocky had seen him had been in the Inverness police station. He needed to make sure that John did not tell Charlie Russell where he was.

Thirty minutes later Jocky agreed to John Urquhart's offer of a job. Importerama, the company where John had been working for seven years, one of the largest import and export companies in Britain, required a chauffeur for the managing director.

The following day John had no recollection of the discussion.

He was surprised therefore when Jocky turned up for work at the Importerama offices a week later.

It cost John an expensive lunch with the Personnel Director before agreement was reached that Jocky Winngate was the ideal candidate for the position of chauffeur.

John just hoped that Jocky was worth the trouble.

He also hoped that the company accountant would not query the exorbitant lunch bill that he had submitted for allegedly entertaining a senior officer in H.M. Customs and Excise.

Jocky just hoped that nobody would ask to see his driving licence.

Nobody had ever asked to see one in Inverness.

CHAPTER FORTY FOUR

NOVEMBER 1974

INVERNESS

Violet Macdonald was standing in the kitchen of Billy Wilson's house in West Drive. The psychologists had all but given up on her. She had good days and bad days. A good day was when she just moped around the house listlessly, not uttering a word even when spoken to. A bad day was when she wandered into the outside world clutching her Varaflame lighter.

There had been no major fires attributable to Violet for several years. Nevertheless at the first sign of smoke her name was mentioned. Even a normal chimney fire brought raised eyebrows and a nodding look.

Violet was doing what she liked best. She was standing in the kitchen of Billy Wilson's house looking out of the window as she washed the breakfast dishes. She always seemed to be in a trance, but more so when executing this task.

She was so deep in thought, a thought that no medical practitioner had ever been able to extract from her, that it was a few seconds before she realised that her eyes were focussed on a movement in the next door garden. She peered intently. She was sure she had seen a movement in the bushes.

A small head popped out from behind the rhododendron bush. It was Tommy Rush, the three year old son of the local scrap merchant. As she looked Tommy ducked down again. Clearly a game of hide and seek was in progress.

The sight of Tommy was the triggering point for Violet to have a headache of migraine proportions. She collapsed on the kitchen floor.

Hearing the thud from the kitchen, accompanied by the

sound of broken crockery, Billy rushed in from the living room. The first thing he saw was Violet on the floor. The next thing he saw was a smashed plate from his mother's best, and only, dinner service. A dinner service which she had proudly taken home one evening from the Harbour Inn. She had received it from a grateful deck hand on a Norwegian vessel. Nobody asked what she had done to deserve his gratitude.

Billy bent down to pick up Violet at the same time as Violet picked herself up from the floor. Their heads collided, adding even more discomfort to Violet. Billy was so thick skinned he barely noticed the blow.

"Are you okay, love?" a concerned Billy asked.

Violet looked at Billy. Her reply was not what he expected.

"I have to go round to my mother's house straight away."

Billy looked at her in alarm. Violet had not been in her family home since she had been released from the mental hospital twelve years previously.

Billy was twenty yards behind Violet as she turned the corner into Kessock Avenue.

"Christ," he thought, "she's running like a bloody mad-woman."

Which was rather ironic, because at that precise moment Violet was more sane than she had been at any time in the previous thirty years.

Violet threw open the gate leading to her mother's house and strode down the path. She rapped on the door.

The door opened and Violet was confronted with her mother, a mother who was much older and feebler than her years. Time clearly had not been kind to her.

Violet gently pushed past her mother and walked straight into the house.

A few seconds later Violet stood at the kitchen window and looked into the rear garden. Billy and her mother looked at her, wondering what she was doing. Violet was unpredictable.

Violet turned. She was smiling.

"God Mum, I've missed you," she said, throwing her arms around her mother.

Mother and daughter stood embracing each other for almost a minute.

Violet broke away from her mother, but still held her hand.

"Could you put the kettle on, Mum, whilst Billy goes to the police-station?" she asked.

Billy stared at her. Clearly she was still not quite right in the head. In fact, not to put too fine a point on it, she was a cornflake short in the packet. Nobody from the Ferry ever went to the police station voluntarily. The only reported instance of this had been in 1934 when Henry MacKenzie had gone there to report his bicycle stolen. He was four years older before he saw his bicycle. The missing four years were spent in Porterfield Prison where he had been detained for burglary offences.

"Give me one good reason why I should go to the nick," Billy said.

"Because I want to report a murder," replied Violet.

Violet had been four years of age at the time of the incident that was to affect her so deeply for so many years. Her father, a military policeman, had been home on leave and was due to return to his unit that night.

It was a late afternoon on a warm day in August 1944. Violet's parents were confident that the war would soon be over and life would return to normal. Sergeant MacDonald would replace his army uniform with overalls and become plain Mr. MacDonald, and return to his job as a foreman plumber with the local council. Violet was playing at "being mothers" and was washing up in the kitchen sink whilst looking out of the window. She noticed her father hiding behind a bush in the neighbour's garden. Then the man who lived next door walked down his path to the Anderson shelter. It was the first time she had seen her neighbour. He was never home a great deal. His wife was always on her own with her young son.

Violet chuckled. She knew that her father was going to jump out of the bushes and shout "boo" at the man next door.

But her father did not move. He just squatted behind the bush watching the man as the man approached the shelter.

The man paused at the door of the shelter. He turned and looked around.

Violet's father crouched deeper into the bushes.

Violet was excited. She could see that if her neighbour kept looking then her father would be found and the game would be over.

Violet banged on the window.

"Daddy," she shouted.

The neighbour turned his head at the sound and looked around. He clearly had no idea where the noise had come from. A few seconds later, apparently satisfied that the noise was not directed at him, he turned and entered the shelter.

Disappointed, Violet stepped off the chair on which she was standing in order to reach the sink and play pretend washing-up. She wandered into the living-room and picked up the doll her father had brought home from England.

Thirty minutes later Violet decided that she would find her dad. She wanted to make sure that he still loved her and he was not too annoyed with her for banging on the window and nearly spoiling his game.

She slipped out of the back door into her garden. Her mother had gone to see her sister who was very ill, and was not expected home until late that evening. Her mother had been quite firm when she had said to Violet "Do not go outside unless your father is with you."

She crawled through a hole in the fence into the neighbour's garden. Slowly she walked towards the shelter at the bottom of the garden. There was no sign of her father or the neighbour.

She stood at the entrance to the shelter. She had been in this type of shelter before. The children played games in them. But she did not like them. They were dark and smelled strange. Like a toilet smell. This shelter was different from the other shelters however. It had a door. A padlock was on the ground by the door.

She thought she could hear a noise in the shelter. But she did not want to upset her dad again by calling to him.

She stepped into the shelter.

A number of boxes were scattered in the entrance to the shelter and prevented her from entering more than two steps.

She peered into the gloom.

She saw her neighbour and her father. They appeared to be having an argument. The neighbour had a spade in his hand. She watched as he raised the spade and struck her father. They were playing at "fighting" just as she had seen the boys do. Playing "war games". They must have given up playing hide and seek.

Very quietly she crept back into the daylight.

Two hours later Violet sat in the living room with her doll. Her father had still not returned, nor had her mother.

She made her mind up. She would go and see if her father and the neighbour had finished playing their game.

Five minutes later she was back in the shelter.

She could barely see the end of the shelter. The daylight from the doorway was fading fast.

But she could see that the ground inside the shelter had been disturbed. As though something or, and here she nearly sobbed out loud, someone, had been buried there.

When her mother returned home that evening, Violet was sitting at the kitchen table playing with a box of matches. The matches were quickly taken away. Violet did not speak all evening. Even when asked where her father was Violet just sat there tight lipped.

Mrs. MacDonald thought it strange that her husband had returned to his unit without saying good-bye. He was not due to leave the house until later that evening. He had promised that he would be there when she returned from visiting her sister. He promised that he would not leave Violet alone.

But Mrs. Macdonald had other thoughts on her mind. Her twin sister had died whilst she had been visiting her.

Violet went to her bedroom. She spent the whole night peering into the next-door garden through a chink in the blackout blind.

Three days later there was still no word from her husband. But Mrs. MacDonald was not too concerned. It was war-time and nothing was normal. She had been surprised to see his uniform laying on top of the bed all neatly pressed, ready for his return to his unit. He must have reported back in civilian clothes. He never was one for letter writing or leaving notes.

But she had her sister's funeral to arrange. There was no time to speculate on where her husband was. She knew that he would get in touch as soon as he could.

Ten days after Mrs. MacDonald had buried her sister the police called at her house. Sergeant MacDonald had not returned to his unit. As far as the authorities were concerned he was missing without leave. He was listed as a deserter.

Twenty four hours after Violet had reported that her father's body was buried in the site of the old Anderson shelter, the police had finished digging the site.

The dig revealed a cache of war-time and post war black market goods. Whoever had hidden the items clearly had no time to retrieve them when the Anderson shelter had been taken down without warning by the council two years after the war had ended. There was no sign of the body that Violet had said would be there.

Twenty four hours after the discovery of the black market material Eckie Jamieson was arrested. Violet had recognised Eckie as the man behind the camera at the South Drive VE Day party. This explained her fear of the camera. She had recognised him again when he was driving the lorry at the harbour in the Algerian Queen incident. The strange thing was that he had not aged. He looked just as he had done twenty years earlier.

It was P.C. Thomson who pointed out that the driver of the vehicle was Ronnie Jamieson and he would only have been seven at the time of the alleged murder. But Ronnie's father Eckie was around at that time. Further investigations revealed that Eckie had been the registered council tenant for the house next to the MacDonalds in Kessock Avenue. He also had a second home in Madras Street. He lived apart from his wife and son. The Kessock Avenue house had clearly been used as the warehouse for a war-time black-market activity.

When interviewed Eckie Jamieson admitted the black market activities but denied that he had a fight with Sergeant MacDonald. The police were still left with the mystery of what had happened to Sergeant MacDonald.

On the face of it he had almost certainly deserted.

A week after the site of the war-time Anderson shelter had been excavated and a degree of normality had been restored, Violet and Billy were sitting in her mother's house.

"I have a present for you, Billy", Violet stated.

She handed Billy the Ronson Varaflame lighter. It was still

in pristine condition.

"I don't think I'll need that again," she said, with a beaming smile on her face.

Two weeks later Billy and Violet were married. They moved in with Mrs. MacDonald.

For the first time in over thirty years Violet was leading a normal life.

She even got over her obsession for John Urquhart.

It was a direct result of the police investigation into Eckie Jamieson and his war-time black market activities that the police uncovered the evidence of his on-going smuggling operation. Eckie was interviewed by two officers from Scotland Yard because of the international implications of the charge. The Algerian Queen was only the tip of the iceberg.

Some of the paperwork impounded by the police mysteriously disappeared. Despite a thorough search by the police lasting several weeks the paperwork could not be found. There was no evidence therefore to tie in Marie Winngate with the smuggling operation.

Eckie was sentenced to fifteen years imprisonment.

Eddie Jamieson was arrested and charged with being one of the ring-leaders in the smuggling operation. The charges also included the distribution of illegal booze to public houses in the Inverness area. He was also charged with being instrumental in the Ferry Battle scam in 1965. The only evidence the police had was that he had a matching two piece suit. But that was good enough for them. Eddie was sentenced to ten years.

Eddie was livid. He fully accepted his punishment for the smuggling racket. But to get sent down for a scam perpetrated by the Nelson brothers was taking things too far. His protestations that the Nelson brothers had been behind the scam was greeted with derision by the police, which was a bit silly. Had they considered the Nelson track record to date, where every job they had attempted had ended in disaster, the Nelson brothers would have been the main suspects for the perpetration of the scam.

But it was much easier to charge Eddie Jamieson. It was another crime off the unsolved list. Of even more importance was the fact that it was another crime off the Ferry unsolved list.

Chief Inspector Berk seized the moment to retire on a high note.

The subsequent reshuffle in the Highland Constabulary resulted in Police Constable David Thomson being promoted to Sergeant.

CHAPTER FORTY FIVE

DECEMBER 1974

INVERNESS

A month after the imprisonment of Eckie Jamieson a patient was admitted to the Inverness psychiatric hospital. The patient was in a distressed state. It was evident that he had been sleeping rough for a number of years. Bizarrely the patient insisted on being called "Sergeant Violet" even though he had no idea what his name was.

It was by pure chance that one of the nurses at the hospital happened to live three doors away from the MacDonald family. She had heard stories about the disappearance of a Sergeant MacDonald during the war years. She knew Violet MacDonald quite well.

That evening the nurse called at the MacDonald house.

A week after being admitted to hospital Peter MacDonald was reunited with his wife and Violet.

It transpired that, on that fateful day in August 1944, having earlier observed strange activities in the next door garden, Sergeant MacDonald had taken it upon himself to keep an eye on Eckie Jamieson. When he tackled Eckie in the Anderson shelter he was struck on the head with a spade. He staggered from the shelter and collapsed in the garden. Violet had passed within four feet of him when she had gone to look for him. When he awoke he had no idea who he was, or where he was. The one thing he could recall was a place called Aldershot and the name Violet. He left Inverness that night. He arrived at Aldershot still none the wiser as to why he was there. By a strange twist of fate he had spent the following ten years working with a plumbing contractor on various Army bases.

It had taken him a further twenty years of wandering the length and breadth of Britain before he returned to Inverness.

CHAPTER FORTY SIX

DECEMBER 1974

INVERNESS

P.C. Hamish Reid and P.C. Hector MacLeod should have been on patrol in the Crown district when the two - way radio between the police station and the police car burst into life. At the time they were listening to the Saturday night horror story on Hector's transistor radio. They were both shaken when a distorted voice cut across the radio dialogue. The play had just reached a very scary moment and both constables were gripping their seats at the time. A shrill scream came out of Hector's mouth on hearing the strange voice within the car. Hamish attempted to reassure Hector by putting his arm around him.

Two minutes later Hamish was still hugging Hector and seemed to be enjoying the experience. Hector was struggling to remove Hamish's arm and at the same time tune in the new experimental radio communication set.

Over the static on the police-radio the faint voice of Sergeant Rob Stewart could be made out.

"Suspected peeping-tom activity in the Crown Drive area. Investigate with caution. And if I find out that you two bloody morons are parked somewhere you shouldn't be I'll have your guts for garters."

The police car was parked in the Woollen Mills car park, three miles from where it should have been. Close enough to get to any emergency in the town. But far enough away from the town to avoid any casual conflict with passing inebriates. It was a Saturday night and the constables had found a parking spot a good two miles away from the nearest public house. It was ten o'clock in the evening on a bitterly cold winter night. Their eight hour shift was due to finish in an hour. So far they had avoided any confrontation with the public. This was mainly due to the fact that they had been parked in the same spot for seven hours.

Ten minutes later Hamish and Hector exited their vehicle. They had driven along Crown Drive but had seen no sign of anything suspicious. Things were normal in the Crown district. The residents were indoors making cocoa.

They were about to leave the area when the flicker of a torch - light alerted the constables to the presence of a man hiding in the bushes, a man wearing a long raincoat and carrying a pair of binoculars.

There was no attempt to resist arrest. The peeping-tom broke down in tears when confronted by the constables.

The peeping-tom case was heard in the Sheriff Court two days later. Sheriff Alastair Horatio Farquharson dismissed the case on the grounds that the accused was a fellow member of the Round Table and could not possibly be guilty of the crime even though he had been caught in flagrante delicto.

Not only was the accused a member of the Round Table, he was a Member of Parliament, and a Conservative one at that. As far as the sheriff was concerned, people do not come more trusting than that.

The explanation that Jeremy Everest gave for his odd behaviour was that he had been checking up on his wife Rosaline who had been leaving the house four evenings a week for the previous twenty months without specifying where she was going. Having seeing her in a compromising position with another man several years earlier, the name Jocky Winngate had not been mentioned since the day of the incident he had reached the end of his tether and had for some time been walking the streets of the Crown district with his binoculars, hoping not to see her with another man, but fearing the worst. It was unfortunate that he had been peering through the window of Councillor Dicky Ryan's home at the time Dicky was entertaining his boy-friend Rodger Thurrock, a regional planning developer.

Rodger Thurrock thought that the peeping - tom was a love

rival and, despite Dicky's protestations to the contrary, had telephoned the police.

At the completion of the court hearing Jeremy tearfully accepted his wife's explanation that she had been working as a volunteer at the Samaritans, specialising in advising people with marital problems.

When he asked her if their marriage would work she gave him the telephone number of the Samaritans. Later that day he telephoned her seeking advice.

On hearing the news of the court case the Conservative Central Office earmarked Jeremy to be a future Prime Minister.

.

CHAPTER FORTY SEVEN

FEBRUARY 1975

LONDON

The back bar of the Fred Lion public house in Victoria Street was heaving with drinkers as John Urquhart and Sandy Roberts fought their way through to find a table. The public house should have been called the Red Lion but due to an error on the part of a clerk in the architect's office the wrong instruction had gone to the developers. By the time the mistake was spotted the gold lettering proudly standing out on the marble fascia of the building could not be changed. Rather than admit an error the architects and brewers concocted a story that Fred Lion was one of the original founders of the brewery.

True to form Sandy was carrying the two pints of beer he had just purchased whilst John fought his way through the throng a few paces in front of him. Sandy had never quite got used to the way John always managed to inveigle his way out of buying the first round of drinks.

The fact that the bar was busy was not unusual, but illegal. It was late afternoon and outside normal licensing hours. The lunch time session had finished two hours earlier. British licensing laws were strict - which explained why all the illegal drinkers were in the back bar of the public house, away from the gaze of passers-by. New Scotland Yard was just one hundred yards along the street. But that did not bother the landlord who was greeting all his customers as friends. The fact that half of them were plain clothes policemen operating out of Scotland Yard eased his mind about breaking the law.

Flying Officer Sandy Roberts had been working at the Ministry of Defence in Whitehall for two months but this was the first opportunity that he and John had to get together to catch up on events. Sandy was off duty and was in civilian clothes. John was supposed to be working but as usual was in the bar. But that was the lifestyle he had adopted. He treated work in civvie street almost as seriously as he had done in the R.A.F.

News from the domestic scene was that Sandy and Jean were living in R.A.F. married quarters at Northolt in west London. John and Susan were still living in their Beckenham flat although they were contemplating a move into deeper Kent. Their three year old son Alex was already talking about "joining the Air Force and being a hero just like his Dad". Recalling the incidents that he and John had got up to whilst they served overseas together, Sandy could not help but wonder what stories John had been telling his young son.

Susan was still working as a lawyer at the legal practice in Lincoln's Inn Fields but in a more senior capacity. Jean was at home looking after her three - year old daughter.

On the Graham front, Leslie was working at Hammersmith Hospital as a surgeon, whilst Alison was a nursing sister at Charing Cross Hospital. Their twin daughters were in the care of their live-in nanny.

The two lads from the Ferry were so intent on gossip that neither of them noticed the tall, heavy built, bearded man giving them strange looks. The man was with the group from Scotland Yard. The man averted his gaze when John looked in the direction of the group.

They were on their fourth pint when John was interrupted by a voice in his ear stating, "The boss wants you back in the office now."

The last person Sandy Roberts expected to see in London, in a chauffeur's uniform, was Jocky Winngate.

"Tell the old git I will be there in a few minutes," John replied.

Jocky looked at Sandy and John.

"Christ," he said, "don't tell me you two are back together again."

"It's a long story," said John, seeing the look on Sandy's face. "Save it for next time."

Jocky walked out of the bar. The eyes of the tall heavy –

built, bearded man followed him. The Scotland Yard man was shaking his head in disbelief.

Fifteen minutes later John Urquhart was back in his office. He glanced out of the window. The bustle of Victoria Street always fascinated him with the constant stream of pedestrians rushing along with their heads down. Commuters rushing to and from the nearby main line Victoria Station.

He could see the front entrance to the Fred Lion from his office window. A small queue had formed with Jocky Winngate at the front, waiting for the front doors to open for the evening session. John wondered how Jocky managed to keep his job. He always seemed to be drinking.

John could not believe the freedom he had in his position. He was encouraged to socialise on a regular basis with his business contacts. What work he had to do could be done in half an hour each day. This consisted of ensuring that the company imports were safely cleared at the docks and delivered within the U.K.

His secretary woke him out of his moment of melancholy.

"The major's still waiting and he's not in a very good mood," was her message.

With a deep sigh John walked out of his office and took the lift to the executive floor. He had met some headcases in his life but his boss Major Bob Stephens, the Head of Security for Importerama, was the biggest nutter.

From experience John knew that any summons from the Major usually meant trouble.

CHAPTER FORTY EIGHT

MAY 1975

INVERNESS

Tommy Ross was desperate for money, which was frustrating for him, particularly as he spent his whole working day with the stuff. As chief clerk at the bank he had responsibility for ensuring the security of the bank strong-room, a strong-room that contained a great deal of money.

Fate decreed that Tommy should find himself in the Harbour Inn on the same evening as the Nelson brothers were working behind the bar. The brothers did not normally work behind the bar but Mary Wilson was in Glasgow on a rare visit to her employers. Mary was short-staffed. The brothers agreed to help out, taking the view that this offer of assistance might put their previous bad experiences with Mary and the Harbour Inn behind them.

It was a particularly busy night with three foreign ships docked in the harbour.

It was the sight of the foreign seamen, and the cash going over the bar, that gave Tommy Ross the idea.

But to make it work he needed some assistance.

He knew the Nelson brothers.

He knew they were incompetent.

He knew they were gullible.

They were perfect for the part.

Terry Nelson was surprised when Tommy Ross offered him a drink. He had always regarded "Tommy" as being a bit of a loner, a man who thought highly of himself, a cut above the normal riff-raff of the area. In fact he was totally out of place in the Harbour Inn. He worked in a bank. Most of the crowd in the area had never been in a bank. Apart from those who attempted the odd break-in.

But one thing Terry had learned at the cradle was never to refuse anything if the price was right. And it did not come any more right than "free".

An exchange of free drinks between Terry and Tommy followed. Terry took the view that he was in charge of the bar as Robbie had been on the customer side of the bar most of the evening with one of the hostesses. As temporary manager Terry felt it was part of his duties to have satisfied customers. This explained the free drinks policy that Tommy had adopted. What Mary Wilson did not see!

It was two o'clock the following morning before Terry got round to discussing business with the brothers.

Mary Wilson could not believe it when, on her return from Glasgow, she was accosted by the Nelson brothers asking if they could help out on any future occasion that she was short-staffed.

Mary agreed.

But only when the pub was very busy, when there were foreign ships in the harbour.

Which was exactly the time that Tommy Ross and the Nelson brothers wanted to work in order to operate their scam.

Three months after the initial meeting between Tommy Ross and the Nelson brothers the scam came to an end.

The idea had been simple. Tommy had noticed that when the foreign seamen were in the bar they drank heavily. They stuffed their change in their pockets. They could have been given anything in their change, particularly if the change was given to them by the Nelson brothers as Scottish ten shilling and one pound notes. The genuine notes would go into the pockets of the Nelson brothers. They had a float of fifty pounds in forged notes in their back pockets, ready to do a swap when the occasion arose. Tommy Ross gave them a regular supply of the forged notes. They split the real notes between them.

The scam would probably have gone on for several months longer had the vessel Hans Andersen not berthed at Inverness harbour after an absence of three months.

Unfortunately for Tommy Ross the Nelson brothers were not behind the bar when the ship docked.

Mary Wilson was behind the bar.

She had just been handed three one pound notes in payment for a round of drinks.

It was the colour of the paper that caught Mary's eye.

Then the print.

Then the realisation that the notes were not only forged, but badly forged at that.

When Mary refused to take the notes there was a muttering of discontent within the bar. The muttering grew to a rumble as the seaman realised that they had been conned. One by one the remainder of the crew of the Hans Andersen produced identical notes.

Inverness had been the only British port of call for the ship in the previous six months.

The Harbour Inn had been the only place they had used.

The money must have had originated from the Harbour Inn.

Mary was in a quandary. The Norwegian sailors were getting restless. They were demanding that she take the money. A riot looked likely.

She took it reluctantly. The last thing she wanted in the pub was a police presence.

The following day she banked it.

At the bank branch she had used for years.

At the Academy Street branch where Tommy Ross worked.

It was not so much a prick of conscience that raised Mary Wilson's concern at what she had done. It was the article in the Herald newspaper stating that forged bank notes had been distributed in the town and that possession of, or an attempt to pass one, could result in imprisonment.

She decided to come clean.

She visited the bank and asked to see the manager.

She explained to him that she may have inadvertently paid in some forged notes the previous day.

The bank manager was surprised. He had received no report

of forged notes from his chief clerk Mr. Tommy Ross. But he did not mind the intrusion. It was not every day that a woman with the style of Mrs. Mary Wilson sat in his office. His mind wandered as he gazed in awe at Mary's low slung blouse and mini skirt.

He decided to visit the strong room to speak to Tommy. And perhaps later that day he might visit the Harbour Inn

Tommy failed to hear the strong room door open. Only he and the manager had a key and the manager never, but never, entered the strong-room.

Tommy was on his second run of forged notes that morning. He had solved the problem of the paper colour and the new notes looked much more genuine. He had had a moment of panic the previous day when one of the tellers had advised him that some suspicious notes had been paid into the bank but he had reassured the teller that he would sort it out. He had taken the forged notes from her and had given her genuine notes in return, in order to make the books balance.

He raised his head from the Letraset printer that he was working on. The bank vault was the ideal place to keep it. Nobody would ever think of looking for counterfeit equipment in a bank vault.

It certainly came as a surprise to the bank manager.

He saw his index linked pension disappearing.

Tommy Ross refused to make any comment to the investigating officers. He went for trial and pleaded guilty. As far as the police were concerned no other parties were involved.

The police had no idea how much forged money was in circulation. There had been reports from Glasgow and Aberdeen of similar notes being passed in dockside hostelries. Mary Wilson confirmed that Tommy Ross had used the Harbour Inn. He had clearly passed the notes over the bar each time he visited. None of the police thought of asking Mary Wilson which staff had been working behind the bar during that time. They would no doubt have been interested to hear that the Nelson brothers were volunteer barmen.

Mary was disappointed when, the day following the arrest

of Tommy Ross, she was informed by the Nelson brothers that they had better things to do with their time than work behind her bar.

CHAPTER FORTY NINE

OCTOBER 1975

INVERNESS

The autumn leaves were falling on the river banks as Sergeant David Thomson glanced through his copy of The Herald. He had been sitting by the river for thirty minutes and was starting to feel the cold air.

It was unusual to read about Marie Winngate in The Herald. The news item stated that wealthy publishing magnate Sir Trevor Dduff had married the former Mrs. Jeffrey Streadman in London. David Thomson recalled Sir Trevor Dduff's name being mentioned in the newspaper several months earlier when he had become the new owner of the newspaper. The editor was clearly keeping in Sir Trevor's good books.

He smiled as he read that the trial of Tommy Ross had drawn to a close - a trial which saw Tommy being sent to prison for eight years. How the hell Ross had expected to get away with trying to pass off counterfeit money printed on a toy printer and without any other assistance was beyond belief.

CHAPTER FIFTY

AUGUST 1977

LONDON

Detective Superintendent Roger Wickson was not amused. In fact he was furious. The biggest smuggling racket in Europe was being controlled from an office only one hundred yards from Scotland Yard. If he looked out of his office window he could even see the bloody office.

"Just how far have we got with this investigation?" he asked, directing the question to the two men sitting opposite his desk.

"We are pretty sure that the whole operation is controlled by the London office," replied the smaller of the two men. "The Dutch and Belgian authorities confirm that this is their finding also."

"So where do we go from here?" bristled the Superintendent.

"If you could give me a bit more time I think that I may be able to make a great deal of progress," replied the bearded heavily built second man.

"What the hell do you hope to achieve in one week that we have not been able to do in thirteen years? Ever since that Algerian Queen fiasco in Inverness", Det. Supt. Roger Wickson concluded, throwing the paperwork on his desk.

"Just trust me please, Super," came the answer from the bearded man who was now standing, stroking his bushy beard as he walked to the window.

"Two weeks then, sergeant, no more" stated the Superintendent, "and perhaps at the end of that week you could also give me an update on the long running saga of this Marie

Winngate, or Lady Dduff, or whatever her present bloody name is. I'll give you ten to one that her present husband kicks the bucket within the next twelve months."

CHAPTER FIFTY ONE

AUGUST 1977

LONDON

A week after Detective Superintendent Wickson had laid down the law at Scotland Yard, John Urquhart was sitting at his desk when his secretary walked into his office.

"There is a call for you on line two," she stated.

"I thought I said that I was not to be disturbed," replied John who was surrounded by paper-work. "I'm trying to make sense of these import documents."

"The caller said you would take it. Something about five pounds you owe him."

John picked up the phone. Who the hell did he owe money to who would telephone him at work? Surely American Express were not chasing him. But even if they were he owed them a great deal more than five pounds.

"John Urquhart speaking."

"Meet me in the back bar of the Fred Lion in five minutes," was the reply before the phone went dead.

John replaced the receiver.

The voice had a faint but familiar accent.

But he had no idea who it was.

Fifteen minutes later John walked into the bar. It was late morning, just before the lunch time crush. Despite the hour, however, there was still about a dozen people in the bar.

He ordered a pint and looked around. There was nobody familiar in the bar.

He had been there ten minutes and was contemplating getting another drink when a pint of beer was placed in front of him. He looked up. A large stocky man with a bushy beard was staring at him.

"Cheers," said the man, "It's been a long time Johnny."

John looked again. He had no idea who the man was. He felt he had seen him somewhere recently - but where?

The large man laughed.

"You have no idea who I am, have you?" said the stranger.

John looked at the man again. The voice was familiar. There was a lilt of Invernessian in the soft accent.

"I'll tell you what. Give me a fiver and I'll put you out of your misery," the stranger said.

"Why on earth should I give you a fiver just to find out who you are?"

"Because you owe me a fiver," replied the man, handing John a folded piece of paper that had faded with age.

John unfolded the paper.

His signature was on it, as was the signature of four of his old school friends.

"Good to see you again John," said Billy Saunders.

John was open-mouthed.

The pair embraced.

"What in heavens name have you been up to in the past - how many years is it?" John asked. "How did you know where I worked? Have I seen you somewhere recently?" The questions tumbled out of John's mouth.

"A bit of this and that. Twenty years. You saw me in here a few days ago," were the replies.

John recalled the tall bearded man in the Scotland Yard group at the bar. The man who appeared to be giving him strange looks.

"Well, it's great to see you again, Billy," said John, "and before we go any further here is the five pounds I owe you."

"Buy me a beer instead," replied Billy. "Who would have thought when we signed that declaration over twenty years ago that we would settle the debt in a pub in London."

"It just shows that we don't know what's around the corner. Sometimes I wish that I was fifteen again when my biggest worry was getting a game of football," stated John.

"As I recall your biggest worry was getting a girl-friend,"

replied Billy. "However, we have things to discuss."

Billy pulled his chair closer to John.

"How much do you know about the organisation you are working for? And in case you think that I am just being nosey, I should tell you that I am a Detective Sergeant with the Serious Crimes team at Scotland Yard."

John looked at Billy in amazement, but before he got the chance to say anything Billy continued.

"Importerama, the company you work for, is a front for the biggest smuggling operation in Europe, possibly the world. We have been after them for a number of years. You may be able to help."

John was trying to take it all in.

"Don't you find that your employers are very generous to you?" Billy asked. "For example, here you are sitting in a pub when most other people would be sitting at their desk. You have a large office, a large salary, a company car, a secretary, and you pretty well do as you please."

It took John a few seconds to grasp just how much Billy knew about him.

"Well," John began in his defence, "I do a good job for them."

"Sorry, John," replied Billy," you do precisely what they want you to do. You liaise with your old mates in Customs and Excise at the docks, which explains why you got the job in the first place. Ask yourself honestly what the hell you know about security to justify getting the job you have."

John thought about what Billy had just said.

It was true. His knowledge of security extended to guard duty in the R.A.F.

"You were employed because some of the staff in Customs who know you from your R.A.F. days are just that bit lax in checking imports that you are responsible for. It also helps that one of the senior Customs officers is on the payroll of Importerama," stated Billy.

John pondered for a few seconds.

It was all true. He could not think of one instance when Customs had queried any of the shipments that he was handling.

For some time he could not believe how lucky he was with

the position he held. The change in his life style had been rather dramatic since he had joined Importerama.

"I would like you to meet my boss," said Billy." But one other thing is bugging me. What the hell has Jocky Winngate to do with your organisation?"

"Jocky is chauffeur to our Managing Director," replied John. "He got the job on my recommendation."

"That could be useful," stated Billy, nodding his head as he did so. "Shall we meet tomorrow at eleven o'clock in the Shakespeare pub down by Victoria Station, there are too many curious eyes in here."

John nodded assent and stood to go.

"Sit down," said Billy. "Get a round in and tell me what you have been up to."

John's head was reeling with what Billy had told him. But he was not too surprised at Billy's comments about Importerama. On the odd occasions he had queried import documentation with Major Bob Stephens he had been told to leave the paperwork with the major. There had never been any feedback on how the query had been resolved.

John and Billy spent the following hour reminiscing. They agreed to meet the following day in the Shakespeare public house.

CHAPTER FIFTY TWO

SEPTEMBER 1977

LONDON

A bomb warning at Victoria Station necessitating the closure of streets in the immediate area resulted in John being thirty minutes late for his meeting with Billy Saunders and his boss. John need not have rushed. The two policemen walked into the Shakespeare ten minutes after John.

"Bloody I.R.A." stated Billy. "They can cause chaos with just a phone-call."

With the introductions out of the way John, Billy, and Roger Wickson settled at a table at the rear of the saloon bar.

"Billy has advised me of your position in Importerama and we are grateful for any assistance you can provide," began the Detective Superintendent. "What we are really after is information on any shipment due to arrive in London soon, particularly from the Far East. Anything you can tell us about delivery points in the U.K. will also assist."

"There is a delivery due from Hong Kong in three days," stated John. "As regards delivery addresses I can let you have a print-out of all deliveries made in the past two years. I keep a copy for my own records. The copy will not be missed."

"What about names of chief contacts in other organisations?" Billy asked.

"That will be a bit more difficult," replied John. "That information is kept in a safe in the Managing Director's office."

"It looks as though we will need a warrant then," Billy stated, looking at the Detective Superintendent.

"No grounds," stated the Dectective Superintendent. "We have no tangible evidence to support the issue of a warrant."

Billy Saunders looked at John.

"Do you have any idea how we can get into the safe?" he asked.

John shook his head.

"Only two people have a key for the safe," he replied, "Mr. Reisling, the Managing Director, and Major Bob Stephens, the Head of Security. The building has manned security on a twenty four hour basis, close circuit television on the ground floor, additional close circuit television on the executive floor, and an electronic key pad system to the doors. It would be impossible to get in undetected."

Billy shook his head.

"Looks like we are stuffed then," he commented.

"Would you get another round of drinks please, Billy? I would like to have a quiet word with John," stated Roger Wickson.

Billy looked at his boss and wondered what he was up to.

Once Billy was safely out of earshot the Superintendent pulled his chair closer to John.

"Does the name Marie Winngate mean anything to you?" he asked.

John nodded, wondering where the conversation was going.

"I've known Marie since she was a child. But what has she to do with Importerama?" replied John.

"Nothing," replied Roger Wickson. "But we have had Marie Winngate under surveillance for some time in connection with the deaths of her husbands. I contacted the Highland Constabulary in Inverness late yesterday to get some more information on her background. It appears that Miss Winngate, or Lady Dduff as she now calls herself, has quite a reputation with the Scottish police."

"I still don't see the connection between Marie Winngate and the Importerama smuggling racket," commented John.

"I dare say if we looked deep enough we would find that some of the goods smuggled into the country over the years have ended up in Marie Winngate's back-yard," stated the Superintendent. "But that is of no consequence. We would only get her for receiving, assuming she was involved. Our interest in Miss Winngate is her father."

"Jocky Winngate?" John spluttered.

"The same. Sergeant Saunders has said that he is working as chauffeur to your top man. He very probably has unlimited access to his boss's office. Jocky Winngate is going to get the information we need out of your Managing Director's safe. As we cannot get a warrant, we need his help."

"But why would Jocky do this for you?" asked John.

"Because if he does not, I shall throw the book at him. The Highland Constabulary have a list of crimes on their books that they would be pleased to see resolved. Mr. Winngate's name has been pencilled in against quite a few of them."

"But if they have the evidence surely the Inverness police would have charged him?" John queried.

"You are right. There is insufficient evidence. But I am sure we can engineer enough evidence to put the frighteners on Mr. Winngate. I suspect that being dragged into Scotland Yard may get him to assist us. Particularly if we state that we shall arrest his daughter for illegal activities if he does not help."

"What kind of illegal activities?" asked John.

"Smuggling, on a small scale. Nothing that we would really bother with unless it was of benefit to us. Can you imagine the reaction of the tabloid press if we arrest Lady Dduff on smuggling charges?"

"What exactly do you want me to do?" asked John.

"Speak to Mr. Winngate. Convince him that it would be in his best interests to assist us. Get him to acquire the documents from the safe."

"Well, I'll try," was John's reply, "although I can't predict his answer."

"Right, let's have another drink," replied the Superintendent, nodding to Billy Saunders, who was standing at the bar waiting for the signal that he could enter into the conversation.

Five minutes later Detective Superintendent Roger Wickson made his apologies. He had more pressing matters to attend to.

"I'll leave you two to finalise things. But I want results soon," was his parting comment.

When Roger Wickson left, John filled in Billy on the

153

discussion he had had with the Superintendent.

Billy was furious.

"I won't pretend that we don't use methods like that, but only with real villains.In this case he was well out of order. Superintendent Wickson has a lot to answer for" Billy commented.

Three hours later John was back in the Shakespeare Bar with Jocky Winngate. Forty-five minutes, three pints of beer and three whiskies later, a furious Jocky stormed out of the bar. He had agreed to help. Not exactly willingly. But he had agreed.

Jocky would have stayed in the bar for a much longer session but he had to go to Heathrow early the following morning to pick up a visitor. The visitor, an important new contact for Importerama, was scheduled to arrive at Terminal One on a flight from Glasgow.

CHAPTER FIFTY THREE

SEPTEMBER 1977

LONDON

The British Airways flight was thirty minutes late arriving at Heathrow. By the time it arrived Jocky Winngate had a pounding headache. It was not the drink from the previous day that was causing the headache. It was the brain effort expounded in planning how to get the documents from Kurt Reisling's safe.

Jocky was so preoccupied in his planning that he did not pay any attention to the arrival of the passengers from the Glasgow flight entering the passenger reception area.

He held aloft the board stating "Importerama".

It was fortunate for Jocky that he noticed the visitor before the visitor noticed him.

At the same moment as Charlie Russell, Jocky's father in law, spotted the "Importerama" sign, Jocky pulled his chauffeur cap firmly over his eyes.

Jocky had forgotten that the flight from Glasgow originated in Inverness.

Despite the efforts of Charlie Russell to engage in conversation with the chauffeur who had picked him up, all he received in reply to his comments was an occasional grunt from the chauffeur.

Charlie gave up trying to be pleasant. He wondered why a company like Importerama employed a surly foreign chauffeur but he had more important things on his mind. At long last he was about to play with the big boys. He had heard rumours on the business grapevine about Kurt Reisling. He was looking forward to doing business with him.

Jocky drove into the underground car-park in the office block housing Importerama. He stepped out of the car and pointed Charlie Russell in the direction of a lift located in the corner of the car park.

Charlie walked towards the lift. He had a briefcase in one hand and an overnight bag in the other.

Charlie made a decision. As soon as he got to know Kurt Reisling a bit better he would have a word with him about his chauffeur.

The moment Charlie entered the lift Jocky telephoned John Urquhart.

Ten minutes later John and Jocky were back in the Shakespeare Bar.

It took Jocky five minutes to outline the problem to John. Charlie Russell was in town. Charlie was about to become involved with Importerama. Charlie had to be warned. Jocky had no grief with Charlie. He just did not want to make Charlie a grandfather.

Which was a great pity, because by this time Charlie's grandson, Jocky and Evelyn's son, was five years old.

John realised that he was the one who would have to tell Charlie. He knew that Charlie was booked into the St. Ermin's hotel that night. The hotel was close to the office. John would visit him at the hotel. But he would have to visit him early in the evening. Charlie, Kurt Reisling and Bob Stephens were booked in for dinner at a West End restaurant later that night.

Seven o'clock that evening found John in the lounge of the St. Ermin's Hotel. He telephoned Charlie Russell's room from hotel reception. Charlie was intrigued when he received a telephone call stating that the Deputy Head of Security at Importerama had important information for him. Charlie agreed to meet the security man in the lounge bar at seven thirty. But he stressed that he could only spare fifteen minutes as he was being picked up at seven forty five by Mr. Reisling's chauffeur.

Jocky Winngate was standing outside the Managing Director's office. He could hear voices inside the room. Major

Bob Stephens was in discussion with Kurt Reisling. Jocky could never quite make out who really was the boss of the outfit. Kurt Reisling was Austrian. The major was English. Jocky had heard rumours about the major - not very nice rumours. Incidents when the major had been in the British Army conducting interrogations and of people disappearing. Jocky had already decided that he would keep his distance from the major.

Jocky had only been standing outside the Managing Director's office a few seconds when the building evacuation alarm sounded.

Being early evening, and after normal office working hours, there were only a few people on the executive floor at the time.

The security receptionist situated just outside the lifts took control. He had just taken a call from the ground floor control room. They had been advised two minutes earlier that there was a suspect car bomb outside the front of their office building. A voice, which the control room telephonist was certain was Irish, said the bomb was due to explode in ten minutes. A physical check outside the building had confirmed that there was a car parked there. The building had to be evacuated. The adjacent New Scotland Yard also had to be evacuated.

As soon as the alarm bells stopped, a tannoy announcement went through the office block advising all staff to leave the premises immediately.

Jocky Winngate had his ear to Kurt Reisling's office door when it burst open and hit Jocky in the face.

Bob Stephens stood there.

He picked Jocky off the floor.

"In here," the major commanded, "we need some help."

Jocky entered the office. His nose was bleeding. It felt as though it was broken.

Kurt Reisling was standing in front of an open safe, stuffing packages into a briefcase.

"Don't just stand there, man," screamed the major, "help me with this briefcase."

Jocky rushed to help the major who was stuffing the second briefcase with the contents from a filing cabinet located under the large desk.

At that moment the security receptionist rushed into the room.

"Sorry, gentlemen, but you have to leave now. Get out of the building immediately."

With both briefcases full they fled towards the rear lift leading to the car-park .

"You must not use the lift," the security man yelled, heading for the staircase.

"Stuff it," replied the major," let's get in the bloody lift and get out of here."

A minute later Jocky and the two executives, who were both wearing dinner suits, were seated in the Daimler.

Jocky's head was pounding. The drink he had consumed during the day had taken its toll. The stress of seeing Charlie Russell was also affecting him. For the first time he realised that not only was his nose probably broken, but there was a cut on his head. He wiped off the blood which was running into his eyes.

Jocky looked up. The security barrier to the car park was raised. He put his foot on the accelerator. He roared up the ramp leading from the underground car park to street level.

His vision was blurred. The blood was still running into his eyes. He could taste the blood in his mouth.

He sped out of the car-park.

Out of the corner of his eye he saw the vehicle bearing down on him.

The bomb disposal vehicle which was rushing to the bomb alert hit the Daimlier side on.

Five minutes later Jocky watched as Kurt Reisling and Major Bob Stephens were loaded into an ambulance. They were both unconscious, and looked as though they would be that way for some time.

Twenty minutes after the collision Jocky entered the St. Ermin's Hotel. He attracted stares as he walked through the reception area with his head swathed in bandages.

He entered the lounge bar.

Charlie Russell and John Urquhart were in deep discussion at one of the tables.

Charlie was about to pick up his brandy when a hand reached in front of him and lifted the glass. Startled, he looked up.

"Hello, Charlie, nice to see you again," said Jocky, as he downed the brandy in one gulp.

"These are for you," was Jocky's next comment which was directed at John, as he handed him the paperwork which he had removed from Kurt Reisling's briefcase.

John Urquhart, Jocky Winngate and Sergeant Billy Saunders stood outside New Scotland Yard. They had just finished a highly successful meeting with Detective Superintendent Roger Wickson.

Peace had been made between Jocky and Charlie Russell. Charlie was grateful for the warning he had received about Importerama.

Jocky was speechless when Charlie produced a photograph from his wallet of Charles Edward Winngate, Jocky's five year old son.

That decided it for Jocky.

He had had enough of London.

He was going to return to Inverness and start his own business.

He had the resources.

He would make a new start.

Marie Winngate, wife of Sir Trevor Dduff, was in deep conversation with her husband about the danger of horse riding, when she glanced out of the car window.

Her chauffeur driven Rolls Royce was just passing New Scotland Yard en route to Heathrow Airport when she saw a sight which made her shake her head. By the time her eyes had relayed the message to her brain the car was one hundred yards further down the street.

She thought she had seen her father talking with John Urquhart. With them was a tall man with a beard. Marie was sure she had seen the man before. She had not spoken to her father since he had left her employment four years earlier, having given her only a week's notice with no indication of where he was going. What was John Urquhart doing in London? And who the hell was the bearded man?

She decided to lay off the coffee. The caffeine was making her hallucinate.

A week after the evacuation of the Impoterama offices Jocky Winngate returned to Inverness. He had plans. But before proceeding with the plans he made his peace with Evelyn and saw his only legitimate son.

It transpired that the car bomb telephone call was a hoax, much to the annoyance of a large number of inconvenienced commuters making their way home.

They were nowhere near as disgruntled as Detective Superintendent Roger Wickson when he found out that a controlled explosion had been undertaken on the new car that had been delivered close to his office in New Scotland Yard in order that he could drive it home as a birthday surprise for his wife.

If he could find the person who had made the call he would crucify him.

He did not hold out much hope.

CHAPTER FIFTY FOUR

SEPTEMBER 1977

LONDON

The odds of ten to one offered by Detective Superintendent Roger Wickson on Sir Trevor Dduff's future existence turned out to be not as generous as first appeared.

Four weeks after declaring his betting book open, the death of Sir Trevor Dduff was announced with a full page obituary notice in The Times. Sir Trevor had died when he had fallen from his horse whilst out riding with his wife in Texas.

Lady Dduff was said to be too distraught to speak to the press.

A post mortem was being held.

Not one to disappoint his troops by doing the unexpected, the Detective Superintendent was in a foul mood when he confronted a weary Detective Sergeant Billy Saunders.

"I asked you a month ago for a report on this Winngate woman. We now have another suspicious death on our hands. It is of no consolation to me that her three husbands to date have died in foreign countries. She is British. Her husbands were British. I wonder who the hell the next poor sod is that she is going to marry. Keep a closer eye on this woman or I'll have your job, sergeant," he thundered.

Billy Saunders turned to walk out of the senior officer's office. There were days when the job was not worth the grief he got.

"By the way, Billy," the Superintendent's voice followed him. "Brilliant work on the Importerama job."

Billy continued walking out of the office. He had a broad smile on his face. There were days when the job was worth the grief he got.

CHAPTER FIFTY FIVE

SEPTEMBER 1977

INVERNESS

In Inverness, Sergeant David Thomson, whose taste in newspapers had gone up-market since being promoted, was flipping through the Times when his eye settled on the obituaries. He cut out the article about Sir Trevor Dduff. It really was time that the Marie Winngate file was taken seriously. He decided to by-pass his immediate superiors and go straight to the Chief Constable with his concerns.

An hour later David Thomson left the Chief Constable's office with a puzzled expression on his face. He had been advised by the Chief Constable that an investigation into the activities of Marie Winngate had been on-going for several years. In view of her national and international connections Scotland Yard had been conducting the investigation. Marie Winngate was of no further interest to the Highland Constabulary. The Chief Constable had been tense throughout the meeting, and had visibly twitched on several occasions. He had been adamant that the constable drop his investigation. He made it quite clear that if Sergeant Thomson did not drop the investigation his future in the force was bleak.

The day following the meeting with Sergeant Thomson the Chief Constable retired from the force on medical grounds.

Meanwhile down at Inverness Castle police station there was a full scale investigation in progress. Somebody had nicked Chief Inspector Wally's copy of the Dandy.

CHAPTER FIFTY SIX

DECEMBER 1977

INVERNESS

Jocky Winngate returned to Inverness in a blaze of glory, and with loads of cash.

Within one month of his return he was the proud owner of three public houses, each one of them operating some form of illegal activity.

Jocky also purchased an interest in a turf accountant business.

He donated (anonymously) one thousand pounds to the local orphanage.

Charlie Russell offered him a position in one of his companies. Jocky declined. He wanted to be his own man.

By the time Jocky had finished setting up his business empire he had expended fifty five thousand pounds.

That still left him with twenty five thousand pounds which was the balance of the money that had been in the packages that Kurt Reisling had removed from his office safe and put in one of his briefcases. He had already given the paperwork from the second briefcase to John Urquhart.

The result had been even more spectacular than Jocky had hoped for.

All he had intended was for Kurt Reisling and Bob Stephens to leave the office during the bomb evacuation. He could then get to the safe for the documents. He knew where the key was kept in the office. He regularly went through all the drawers in the office when he was kept waiting whilst the managing director was at a board meeting. Kurt Reisling kept some good cigars. He never had missed the odd one. It had been a stroke of luck when the two executives had rushed out of the office with the briefcases – not to mention the car crash.

Jocky had been slightly miffed when the security guard had said that he was Irish. But with the amount of drink Jocky had consumed that day it was a wonder that he had been understood at all. Still, it made the call sound more authentic.

It was encouraging to hear that the Importerama directors would probably be in prison for twenty years. Out of sight - out of mind.

The icing on the cake was the news that the car Jocky had picked as the suspect bomb vehicle, the one he had spotted on the street, the one whose number plate he had passed to the security staff, happened to belong to that arrogant English git Detective Superintendent Roger Bloody Wickson.

Jocky was sitting in the MacEwans Arms. He had considered putting in an offer for the pub but he needed somewhere to drink where Evelyn would not find him. He was avoiding the Harbour Inn for a few weeks as Mrs. Mary Wilson had become a complete pain in the neck. All she talked about was the fact that her daughter Mary junior had gone into a retreat. Apparently Mary junior had never quite got over her non-existent affair with John Urquhart. This was nothing to do with Jocky but Mary senior felt that Jocky had a sympathetic ear. Had she been forty years younger he probably would have.

Jocky picked up his pint.

"Cheers, lads" he toasted, as he raised his glass to the Nelson brothers, "We're back in business."

CHAPTER FIFTY SEVEN

JUNE 1982

LONDON

Flight Lieutenant Sandy Roberts stood in the signals office in the Ministry of Defence building in Whitehall. As officer in charge of communications traffic he had responsibility for the security and decoding of all incoming signal traffic.

Sandy glanced through one of the signals he had been handed by the signals office N.C.O. The signal had already been decoded. It made reference to a mission that had been undertaken by an S.A.S. team in the Argentinian occupied Falkland Islands.

The signal read:-
TOP SECRET
Operational Immediate
DTG 220800Z
From:- Alpha Roger Echo One Four
To:- Invincible
copy MOD London attention G20
copy OC 22 S.A.S. Hereford
SITREP - Helicopter from unit placed unit at drop zone. Proceeded to final rendezvous where close target recce undertaken on enemy positions. Mission to destroy signalling station successful. Engaged in heavy LMG exchange. 2 i/c killed in action which followed. Assistance required. Lying up points as drop zone.

Message Ends.

From previous experience Sandy knew that H.M.S Invincible would have already picked up the S.A.S. team using one of their Sea King helicopters.

He placed the signal in the pigeon hole. There was no need for any further action on his part.

Sandy picked up the next signal and began to read.

Sergeant Tommy Burns, Parachute Regiment, on attachment to the S.A.S., lay back in the webbing seat in the Sea King helicopter. It had been a tough mission. Losing his second - in - command had been a blow.

He was due on leave the following week. He would be glad to have a few days in Inverness with Loraine and the kids.

CHAPTER FIFTY EIGHT

SEPTEMBER 1982

LONDON

John Urquhart was conscious of the man staring at him. He had seen him in the wine bar on a previous occasion. Placing his gin and tonic on the bar counter John raised himself from the very comfortable bar-stool. It was time for a closer inspection of the stranger. The gents toilet was directly behind where the stranger was sitting.

His attempt at being discreet was a dismal failure. Direct eye contact was made as John sauntered past the man. The stranger smiled.

"Just my luck, a bloody queer," John muttered to himself. "I just hope he does not follow me."

Three minutes later John exited the gents. His fears at being followed and being propositioned were unfounded. But the stranger gave him a big grin as he walked past.

A minute after John had resumed his seat at the bar the stranger introduced himself as Bob Parker, architect and man about town.

Lady Georgina Leader was no lady. That was obvious even to John, even though it was the first time in his life he had ever held a discussion with a woman of title.

Looking at John, over the shoulder of Lady Georgina, towered the figure of the chairman of Kiploch Investment Management. The only reason he was not also having a go at John was because he could not get a word in. Lady Georgina had been lambasting John for five minutes. From previous experiences the chairman knew that the tirade could go on for another ten minutes. He himself had been on the receiving end of her tongue on more than one occasion.

John had been working at the head office of Kiploch Investment Management for five years, since the enforced closure of Importerama. As Head of Property Services he had responsibility for the day to day operation of the company property portfolio.

Three weeks earlier he had been asked to produce a report indicating the refurbishment requirements for the head office for the following budget year. Within this report he was instructed to make any recommendations necessary for the upgrading of the offices. In making the request the chairman of the company specifically had in mind the need to upgrade the information technology equipment, to ensure that the investment management company was at the forefront of new technology. As one of the brand leaders in their field of expertise, they were keen to keep ahead of American and European rivals.

In typical John Urquhart fashion, John crashed into his task. He knew just the man - Bob Parker. The same Bob Parker he had met the previous month in Balls wine bar. John was still unsure about Bob's sexuality. But he was a damn good drinking companion.

Eighteen days after the initial request the report was complete. Bob Parker submitted the report direct to the chairman's office. Three days later, having flown back from New York on receipt of a vitriolic precis of the report by fax from the original designer of the head office, who happened to be Lady Georgina Leader, Terence Beechwood, the chairman of Kiploch, arrived back in his office. Ten minutes later John received a command. "Report to the chairman's office at four o'clock this afternoon with architect Mr. Robert Parker, the initiator of the report". The message from the chairman's secretary also stated that the chairman could not care less if Mr. Parker was at his mother's funeral, or even his own funeral. Just make sure he was at the meeting.

Bob Parker, on receipt of this request from John, made himself available. It was not too inconvenient for him. The Kiploch job had been the first bit of work he had in eighteen months, ever since he had been involved in the design project for the proposed Channel Tunnel. He had seen nothing wrong with his concept of a roller - skating lane running alongside the rail tracks going through the tunnel. After all, what is architecture and design if not innovative?

John arranged to meet Bob Parker in the same wine bar they had first met.

John arrived at the wine bar at three o'clock, which gave them an hour to discuss the report before seeing Terence Beechwood. The bad news was that Bob, with nothing else to do, had arrived at the wine bar two hours earlier.

Within forty five minutes of John's arrival the report had been thrashed out. John reminded Bob that he had not seen the report. "What precisely did it contain that had caused so much furore?" Bob assured John that the proposals were sound and would lead to a better working environment for Kiploch staff. But rather than repeat himself John should wait until the meeting and they would run through the proposals with the chairman. Bob was adamant. The proposals were sound. In fact after two bottles of wine he convinced John that they were damn good.

At four o'clock John and Bob Parker walked into the chairman's private meeting room, the one reserved for meetings with statesmen and heads of large international corporations. The room had an old fashioned air about it, with oak panelled walls, oil paintings and valuable loose items, which gave the room an air of stability and wealth. This was a room where business could be conducted in the knowledge that whatever business Kiploch was being entrusted with was in safe hands.

Terence Beechwood and Lady Georgina Leader were seated around the conference table. But before John and Bob Parker had the chance to sit down the chairman and Lady Georgina walked out of the room. The chairman gestured for John and Bob Parker to follow him.

The twentieth floor of Kiploch House, the floor they were walking round, comprised six rooms, all designed for client meeting and entertaining. Each of the rooms was designed in the same style as the chairman's private meeting room. The view of London, spread out below, was spectacular.

Ten minutes after the inspection had begun the party were back in the private meeting room. Not a word had been spoken during the tour of inspection. A tour which had consisted of the chairman opening the door to each one of the rooms, ushering the party inside, and then standing for a few moments whilst he surveyed the interior of the room. Two of the rooms were being used at the time. The chairman seemed oblivious to the meetings being held.

The opening comment from the chairman's mouth was not encouraging.

"Can you think of one good reason why I should not fire you?"

John looked up, hoping the question had not been directed at him.

It had been.

It was not quite the comment that John had expected to hear.

Something like "an excellent report" or even "well done" would have been preferred.

John looked at his chairman, who was clearly seething with anger.

"What in heavens name possessed either of you two cretins to submit a proposal that this company convert the client floor of this building, the bloody rooms we've just looked at, into a sushi bar in order to bring in extra revenue? Who the hell do you think you are working for? Trust House Forte?"

John saw the flaw in Bob's proposal straight away.

It was at this point that Lady Georgina, the original designer of the Kiploch House project, blew her top.

Fifteen minutes after the chairman's opening comment John and the rest of the party stood in the lift lobby of the twentieth floor. Lady Georgina was in the sixth minute of her observations on the incompetence of "the two biggest morons she had ever encountered"- namely John and Bob Parker. Her screaming voice could still be heard as the chairman ushered her into his meeting room. To the disappointment of the team from Tokyo Bank who had been concluding a deal in one of the rooms. A deal that was successfully concluded when the Japanese over-heard that a sushi bar was being installed in the building, and that Trust House Forte had purchased Kiploch Investment.

Lady Georgina's final comment to Bob Parker was "Call yourself an architect?"

To which Bob replied "Call yourself a lady?"

The chairman's office door had just closed when Bob, in a drunken stupor, slid down the wall he had been leaning on, dislodging a valuable oil painting on the way.

It took John five minutes to get Bob into the lift.

Five minutes in which he prayed that the door to the chairman's office would not open.

Ten minutes later John and Bob were back in the wine bar. John was deeply depressed. Bob was sitting at the bar with a bottle of champagne and a grin on his face.

"I don't know what's making you so pleased," was John's opener. "I've probably lost my job and your reputation is up the spout."

Bob Parker picked up the fluted glass and savoured the champagne.

John thought he misheard when the word "revenge" was uttered by Bob.

But he did not mishear when Bob uttered the word again.

"What do you mean, revenge? What has Kiploch done to upset you?"

"It's not Kiploch. It's you I can't stand, you cretin."

John stared at Bob dumfounded.

"What the hell have I done to you?" John spluttered.

"R.A.F El Adem, 1958. Remember it?" was Bob Parker's reply.

"How could I forget that hell-hole?"

"You were on guard-duty over a crashed Canberra. Thanks to your incompetence the orderly officer was called out." Bob stated.

"You were the orderly officer?" queried John.

"No. I was the station headquarters clerk who was with the orderly officer that afternoon. We were half way through a bottle of port when we were interrupted, thanks to your stupidity. Another ten minutes and I would have persuaded him to leave the R.A F and set up home together."

John's mind flew back to the grim days in the Libyan

Desert. He recalled several run-ins with the records clerk but had never actually met him.

"I thought it was you the moment I set eyes on you last month," stated Bob Parker. "The moment I heard you order a drink in that stupid Scottish accent I was definite."

Bob Parker had the champagne flute to his lips when John hit him. He completely missed the target of Bob's face but connected with his shoulder. It was enough to send Bob tumbling to the floor.

John walked out of the wine bar without turning round.

CHAPTER FIFTY NINE

APRIL 1987

LONDON

Terence Beechwood assumed that "the moron Urquhart" had been fired. It had been five years since the sushi bar incident and not once had he seen Urquhart in his wanderings around Kiploch House. Nor was there any sign of him at the staff Christmas party.

But John had not been fired. He had been promoted - sideways. He was given responsibility for the maintenance of the company Business Continuity Plan. The Director of Personnel had some degree of sympathy with John. He also had previous dealings with Lady Georgina.

John had a new work place. In White Hart House, a satellite office located two hundred yards from Kiploch House. He had his own office, although it could have been more aptly described as a broom cupboard. Provided there was no industrial Hoover to be stored. At eighty square feet of office space there was just enough room for a desk and a filing cabinet.

But he was his own master. Provided that he ensured that the Continuity Plan was up to date and that the future of Kiploch Investment management was secure

As luck would have it, the plan was never tested.

John Urquhart walked out of the meeting with a raging headache. The meeting had lasted longer than expected. It had been convened by the City of London Disaster Recovery Team to give an update on I.R.A. activities. There had been more than forty attendees, which meant that there would be a run on headache tablets that afternoon, or large gin and tonics.

The news was not good. There were clear indications that an I.R.A. cell was active. There was the possibility of an incident at any time.

It was a time of crisis, and John reacted the way any Ferry lad did in a crisis.

Fifteen minutes after the meeting had finished he found himself in The Green Man, one of the less salubrious public houses on the fringe of the City. But being the type of pub that it was, John knew that there would be no City high-fliers there.

He had no meetings that afternoon. He could be contacted by bleeper if there was anything urgent. He just needed an hour on his own.

The Green Man was virtually empty when he walked in. There was just one solitary punter sitting at the bar.

John sat on a bar stool and picked up his pint.

The background music was good. Dean Martin. Somebody had taste.

John was back in Malta. It was 1959. He was listening to Dean Martin singing Volare on a jukebox in a little bar in Valletta. Just before he and Sandy Roberts had boarded the Royal Navy ship H.M.S. Eagle.

The memory raised a smile. It was strange how time erased bad memories. He had hated his time in the Libyan Desert. Somehow it no longer seemed so bad.

He was suddenly aware that somebody was talking to him. He looked up.

The stranger at the bar repeated the question.

"Is that a Caley tie you're wearing?"

John looked at the stranger. He then looked at his tie. He had put it on that morning without thinking. He had received the Inverness Caley F.C. tie as a Christmas present from his brother James several years before.

"It's a Caley tie all right. But how in heavens name did you recognise it?"

"I'm an old Caley fan myself," came the reply, "originally from the town but I've lived in London for the past thirty years. I'm Donnie Bolton."

John looked at Donnie Bolton. The name rang a faint bell.

"I used to know a Bolton family in Laurel Avenue," John

commented.

"The very same," replied Donnie.

An hour later the gossip had run out. The reminiscing was complete. Donnie was an old friend of John's brother James.

"There's a club near here," stated Donnie. "I think you would enjoy it. An Inverness woman runs it."

John looked at his watch. He checked his bleeper. No messages. It had been a long time since he had relaxed. In for a penny............

Donnie strode into The Penguin Club. It was evident that he was a regular there by the way he was greeted by the girls. Girls wearing very little. John followed behind. He was having second thoughts about the visit to the club.

"I'd like you to meet Norma," Donnie stated, introducing John to a very attractive woman. It was not just her physical attraction that made her stand out. She was the only woman in the club wearing more than underwear. "Norma is the manager here."

"Norma, this is Johnny Urquhart from Inverness, our old stomping ground," said Donnie, completing the introductions.

"Well well, so we meet again, Johnny," said Norma.

"Have we met before?" asked John.

"Oh, we've met before. I was only thirteen at the time. Norma Wallace. Remember me?"

John looked at the woman. Realisation came flooding back. Norma Wallace, the young girl who had been his next door neighbour, the young girl who had received a pornographic magazine which John had sent to his brother James, the Norma Wallace who at the age of thirteen had taken up stripping and who had gone into strip club management.

Norma put her arm around John.

"I think I owe you a drink, Johnny. Were it not for you I would probably be stuck in Inverness with some idiot of a husband and four or five kids."

Three hours later John left The Penguin Club.

He arrived home by taxi four hours later than normal.

He had only been home ten minutes when Susan arrived home. She was full of apologies. She had been sitting on a train for four hours outside Victoria Station due to a major points-failure at Herne Hill. It never entered her head to enquire how John had managed to get home. It was just as well. John had his head in the Evening Standard. Had Susan not been busy preparing a late supper, she would have heard a soft snoring from behind the newspaper.

.

CHAPTER SIXTY

JULY 1987

LONDON

Ten years after the death of her husband Sir Trevor Dduff, Marie Winngate met Lord Peter Castello whilst she was attending a gala performance of Swan Lake at the Royal Opera House.

Five weeks later readers of the society column in the Daily Express were advised that the couple had tied the knot at the private church located in the grounds of Lord Castello's Buckinghamshire estate and immediately after the wedding ceremony they had flown to New York on honeymoon.

Had the new Lady Castello bothered to look four seats behind her on the Concorde flight, to New York she would have been surprised to see the same bearded man that she had seen talking to her father outside New Scotland Yard ten years earlier.

Detective Inspector Billy Saunders was under orders. Make sure that the New York police are informed that Lord and Lady Castello are in town. Monitor their movements. All the evidence to date indicated that, although nothing definite could be established, the long arm of co-incidence had stretched a bit too far in the so called accidental deaths of Marie Winngate's previous three husbands spread over a period of twenty five years.

Lord Castello was related to the Royal Family. Heads would roll if this husband died suddenly, other than through a heart attack witnessed by several people, with Marie Winngate being a thousand miles away at the time.

CHAPTER SIXTY ONE

SEPTEMBER 1989

LONDON

Lord Peter Castello died in his swimming pool in the early hours of the morning. The news was the main headline in most of the tabloid press. There was intense speculation on the cause of his death by one or two of the gutter press, one of which described the bereaved Lady Castello as "a woman with a dubious background, having being raised in a council estate in Scotland, but as the result of the deaths of four husbands in strange circumstances, she was now one of the wealthiest women in Britain."

Billy Saunders, with one month left to serve in the police force before compulsory retirement, was put in direct charge of the enquiry. He chose not to interview Marie. There was no point in it. The cause of death according to the coroner was a heart attack whilst swimming. Certainly the timing looked odd. Three o'clock in the morning was not the conventional time to take a dip. But the evidence was irrefutable.

Billy Saunders submitted his final report.

His report stated that although the four husbands of Marie Winngate had all died in strange circumstances there was no firm evidence that there had been foul play. The fact that she was a very wealthy person as a result of these deaths was no reason to assume that she had a hand in their deaths.

A decision was taken.

The file at Scotland Yard was closed.

But the question was on everyone's lips.

Would there be a fifth husband?

CHAPTER SIXTY TWO

OCTOBER 1989

LONDON

Sandy Roberts had retired from the R.A.F with the rank of Squadron Leader and had been in civvie street two years. He was the Director of Operations at International Finance Limited, an American owned finance company located in the heart of London's financial district, close to John Urquhart's office.

Despite having been in the Royal Air Force over thirty years, during which time he had served in many countries and with many nationalities, Sandy had great difficulty working with his American bosses.

The work was demanding, more demanding than any task Sandy had ever undertaken before. International Finance had a strict work ethos.

Sandy was in his office when he received a telephone call from John. He had just enough time to register the fact that John had invited him to Blacks Club for someone's retirement celebration before he rushed off to the boardroom for a conference call with the Houston head office. He arrived in the conference room to find that the conference call had begun. Paul Rodgers, Sandy's boss and the European Chief Executive of the organisation, was chairing the meeting. Sandy got on quite well with Paul Rodgers. For an American he wasn't bad company and Sandy and he frequently had a drink together after work.

The conference call finished on time, which in itself was a change. Sandy had often been detained in the office until late in the evening due to a scheduled thirty minute conference call lasting three hours. There was more chance of hell freezing over than getting a decision from Houston.

Sandy collected his papers together at the end of the call. He looked at his watch. John had given him the address of the restaurant. The name rang a bell. Blacks Club, one of the better clubs in the city. A drink with John was what he needed.

He was suddenly aware that Paul Rodgers was holding him by the arm.

"What are you doing for lunch, Sandy?" asked Paul.

"As it happens I'm meeting an old friend."

Paul Rodgers looked at Sandy.

"Can we have a five minute chat in your office?"

Sandy nodded, wondering what the head man wanted with him.

Two minutes later they were sitting in Sandy's office.

"I need some advice," was the surprising opener from Paul, "and I don't know who else to speak to. You seem a pretty worldly guy. You've been around quite a bit."

"Advice, what kind of advice?" asked Sandy, looking at his watch discreetly.

"Well, it's a man to man thing." Paul hesitated before he continued. "I think that my wife is having an affair. She is out of the house a great deal and she is much younger than I am. I found a lot of strange looking underwear in our bedroom whilst I was looking for my cuff-links the other day. I don't know who to speak to. If I mention it to any of my American colleagues I would not be surprised to find myself on the next flight back to Houston. The company is very strict about the image projected by the directors. I just don't know who to turn to."

Sandy looked at Paul. This was the last thing he had expected to hear.

"I'm not quite sure what to say," Sandy commented.

"Sorry, Sandy," replied Paul Rodgers standing up, "I just felt the need to talk to somebody about it. Somebody I could trust."

Sandy looked at the concerned look on the face of the top man in his company.

"Look, Paul, why don't you join my friend and me for lunch. A bit of company might help you."

"Great idea Sandy, thank you. Where are you going?"

"Blacks Club," replied Sandy. "I've never been there but I

have heard of it."

Had Sandy looked at Paul he would have seen a startled look on his face. Paul had definitely heard of Blacks Club.

"Blacks Club it is, then," Paul stated.

"We'll take a taxi," said Sandy. "I'll get one on the company account. See you in reception in five minutes,"

Five minutes later the Computacab taxi pulled up outside the offices of International Finance Limited.

Sandy handed the driver the piece of paper on which he had written the address that John had given him.

The driver looked at Sandy.

"Are you sure this is right guv?"

"Certainly," replied Sandy. "I had the message repeated three times."

"Okay guv. You're paying the bill."

"Not quite," replied Sandy. "It's on our company account."

"As you say guv," was the reply.

The absence of lunch breaks and the frequent late evening working meant that Sandy was not familiar with the city area of London. Paul Rodgers knew the geography even less. Apart from the odd drink with Sandy in the city wine bars he had only seen the inside of the office and his home in the year he had been in London. He and his wife were not hitting it off. He could hardly blame her if she had found another man. He had not been too demonstrative with her lately. He vowed that at the first opportunity he would show her just how much he still loved her.

Sandy was intrigued by the route that the cab driver was taking. Then he saw the street sign "Commercial Road". It was on the edge of the City area. He looked around. The area was a bit seedier than he had expected.

The cab stopped. The driver pointed.

"There you are guv, Blacks Club".

Sandy looked at the building the taxi driver had pointed to.

"Are you sure this is the right place?" he asked.

The driver handed Sandy the slip of paper with the address on.

It was the correct address.

Sandy and Paul got out of the cab.

Blacks Club was a dingy looking place. The front door was closed. The windows were painted black.

Sandy approached the door of the club and pushed.

He stepped into a haze of smoke and dope.

Paul was pushing him from behind. He wanted to see what Blacks Club was all about. He wanted to know why his wife had a visiting card from Blacks Club.

Ten feet into the club Sandy saw John Urquhart. He was standing talking to a tall very attractive well dressed woman and a large bearded man. The woman appeared to be quite a bit younger than John.

John caught Sandy's eye and called him over.

"Let me introduce you to our hostess," he said to Sandy.

Sandy looked at the woman. She was a stunner.

"This is Norma Wallace," John stated.

"I remember you, Sandy. I had a bit of a crush on you when you lived in Inverness" the woman stated.

Sandy looked at her.

Realisation flooded him.

Norma Wallace. Of course he remembered her. But was there not something about her leaving her home town under a cloud? Something to do with John and his brother James? He would have to get John to remind him of the details.

"What are you doing here?" Sandy asked Norma.

"I run this place. I also run three other clubs. I'm surprised John has not mentioned them before. He has been in each one of them," replied Norma.

Sandy looked around him. Blacks Club was not what he had envisaged. Then it dawned on him. Browns Club was the name of the exclusive dining club he had been thinking of.

Sandy looked at Paul Rodgers. What the hell was his boss going to make of this?

But Paul Rodgers was in another world.

Paul was looking at the pole dancer on a small stage.

She was being gazed upon by a couple of dozen leering men.

She was scantily dressed.

But Paul recognised her.

He had seen the thong she was wearing when he had been looking for his cuff links. At the same time as he had seen the calling card for Blacks Club.

His wife had not found another admirer.

She had found dozens of them.

Whilst Paul was coming to terms with his wife's hobby, Sandy was being introduced to Billy Saunders. Sandy and Billy had not met for more than thirty years.

It was Billy's final week in the police force. It had been John's idea that they all meet in Blacks Club for lunch.

John, Sandy, Billy, and Paul, left Blacks Club three hours later. They were all drunk. Once Paul had got over the initial shock of seeing his wife displaying her assets he relaxed and had a few drinks. Then a few more. He made the peace with his wife. He was relieved that she did not have a lover.

Sandy and Paul made a vow. Nobody at International Finance must ever know that the European Chief Executive and his Director of Operations had spent the afternoon in a pole dancing club.

There was no reason why anybody at International Finance should find out.

Until an over zealous accounts clerk, who knew all the shady haunts of the East End, refused to pay the taxi bill for a cab hire from the office to Blacks Club. It was inconceivable that a senior executive of International Finance would visit Blacks Club.

The taxi company wrote to the Company Secretary of International Finance demanding payment.

The Company Secretary looked into the matter.

A week later the matter was the topic of conversation in Houston.

Paul Rodgers suddenly found that he was more popular than he had realised.

But not half as popular as his wife was.

CHAPTER SIXTY THREE

NOVEMBER 1989

INVERNESS

Marie Winngate was surprised and delighted to receive the call from her organisation in Glasgow. She had been considering disposing of her Inverness business interests for some time in order to concentrate on her world wide real estate. Out of the blue someone had offered to buy the five public houses in Inverness for fifty thousand pounds.

Marie put a conservative estimate on the value of the pubs at seventy five thousand pounds. But the chance of finding a single buyer for all five public houses had seemed unlikely. She was prepared to take a loss in order to finally get rid of the Inverness business connection.

Three weeks later Marie disposed of her interests.

The day after the transaction was finalised Billy Saunders carried out a tour of inspection of his new business venture. He had some firm ideas about the management of the pubs.

One thing was certain. At some stage he had to get rid of Mrs. Mary Wilson from the Harbour Inn. She was well past her sell by date.

But the two new managers looked promising. They were both on the old side. But they assured him they had some knowledge of the pub trade.

Terry Nelson was put in charge of the Merkie Bar.

Robbie Nelson took over management of the Auld Lang Syne.

CHAPTER SIXTY FOUR

MAY 1990

INVERNESS

The death of Mrs. Mary Wilson should have been no surprise to her regular customers at the Harbour Inn. Mary had experienced a new lease of life when Billy Saunders had taken over ownership of the public house six months earlier. Despite some initial reservations from Billy about her management style, and her age, Mary had proven him wrong.

It was the way Mary died that caused the eyebrows to be raised.

Mary was seventy seven years of age when she died of cardiac failure following an evening of merriment in the Harbour Inn with the crew from a Norwegian freighter. The session lasted eight hours.

CHAPTER SIXTY FIVE

AUGUST 1990

INVERNESS

It was in the Auld Lang Syne that Eddie Jamieson came seeking his revenge on the Nelson brothers.

Terry Nelson stood at the bar in deep conversation with his brother Robbie. An eavesdropper would have heard the words "cheap", "safe", and "he'll never find out".

It was the scream from the barmaid that awoke the brothers from their discussion.

Terry and Robbie looked at the girl, then followed her gaze.

Eddie Jamieson was standing ten feet away from them holding what appeared to be a sawn off shotgun.

"Must be my lucky day," was Eddie's opening gambit.

"Hello, Eddie. I take it that you've been released?" was Terry's reply.

The shotgun blast took part of the ceiling down.

"The next shot will be for real," stated Eddie.

Meanwhile, in the street outside, the police car that had been on routine patrol heard the sound of the shotgun.

"Quick," P.C. Hamish Reid called to his colleague P.C. Hector MacNab, "put your foot down."

"Where to? Where did the shot come from?" replied Hector, who was new to the Ferry district.

"Drumnadrochit," replied Hamish Reid. "Let's get the hell out of here."

Thirty minutes later Hamish and Hector were ten miles away in a lay-by on the Loch Ness road having a cigarette.

"Christ, that was a close one," Hamish stated.

By this time Eddie Jamieson had the situation well under

control in the Auld Lang Syne.

Terry and Robbie were cowering behind the bar.

Eddie was on his fourth whisky.

There was nobody else in the bar. Like seeds to the wind, the drinkers had dispersed at the sight of Eddie with a shot-gun.

Eddie had heard all the explanations he was prepared to take. He tried to think of one redeeming feature about the brothers but none came to mind. For thirty years they had been a thorn in his side. Every thing he had asked them to do had ended in disaster.

The door of the pub opened just as Eddie reached the end of his deliberations. He had decided that the brothers were not worth another spell in prison.

It was Eddie's little sister Elsie who walked into the bar, although the word "little" could no longer apply.

He did not recognise her at first. It had been over thirty years since she had disappeared overnight with her American airman. He had no idea that she had returned to Inverness whilst he was in prison. He had no idea that the death of her husband had prompted her return.

The siblings looked at each other. Eddie did not know whether to hug her or shout at her.

Terry broke the silence.

"Elsie darling, you look terrific," he exclaimed.

Elsie looked at Terry Nelson. She had only ever spoken to him once in her life. She tried in vain to recollect his name.

It was Robbie who caused the damage.

"Go on, Nappy. Give her a cuddle," he said, before it dawned on him what he had called Eddie.

"I'll bloody Nappy you," screamed Eddie lifting the shotgun.

"Don't be a bloody fool," Elsie screamed. "Put the gun down. What the hell has come over you?"

Eddie looked at her and lowered the weapon. It dawned on him that she had no idea that he had spent years in prison because of the Nelson brothers and their Battle of the Ferry scam.

Eddie placed the weapon on the bar.

"Come here, love," he said to Elsie.

He hugged Elsie and whispered to her. She looked at him. After a few seconds she nodded, in apparent agreement with what he had said.

Elsie walked out of the pub.

"Right, now for some action," Eddie stated, walking towards the Nelson brothers.

It could have been worse.

Both brothers were off work for a week.

But the bruises eventually disappeared.

A week later Eddie was charged with being in possession of a firearm without a licence. A public spirited citizen, visiting the Ferry district, and totally ignorant of their ways, had called the police station reporting the gunfire. The station was unable to raise the patrol car as it was out of radio contact. Three squad cars were sent to investigate.

Eddie's solicitor Stuart Hutchinson put forward a plea of "not guilty", stating that Eddie had found the weapon in the street. He had entered the bar to use their telephone to call the police to report the find, but he had slipped on the floor and the gun had gone off accidentally. This account could be confirmed by the manager of the Auld Lang Syne Mr. Terry Nelson, who unfortunately was too ill to attend the court as a witness as he had injured himself slipping on the same piece of flooring as Mr. Jamieson.

The sheriff was comforted by the fact that the public house was now owned by an upstanding member of the community, Mr. Billy Saunders. After all Mr. Saunders had been a high flyer at Scotland Yard, and was already firmly entrenched in the local masonic circle, and was also a member of the Round Table.

The sheriff had overlooked one thing however.

Billy Saunders had been taught at the old Kessock Primary School where pupils graduated either as a master in criminal activities, or as a certified lunatic.

Billy Saunders was no head-case.

After thirty years in the police force he knew every racket going.

CHAPTER SIXTY SIX

JULY 2002

INVERNESS

John was at work when he was given the news of the death of his brother James. At the age of sixty nine James experienced cardiac failure whilst he was playing dominoes in his local pub.

John and Susan returned to Inverness for the funeral.

John was philosophical. He had been part of a large family, a family that would get smaller as time passed. He was simply grateful that he had known James as a brother.

John visited the grave of his parents and the homes in which he had lived as a child. He stood outside the house in which he had lived during his teenage years. Nearly fifty years had passed since he had helped his father in the garden. He could still smell his mother's baking.

John and Susan stayed at the New Caley Hotel. Their bedroom window overlooked the River Ness. Across the river John could see the old cinema where, in his early teens, he had spent so much of his time watching Doris Day musicals, time that should have been spent in a class-room.

They walked through the Ness Islands.

It was a beautiful summer day.

John looked at the dance area where he had spent so many evenings as a youth.

The bandstand and the dance floor was now a mound of earth.

He was not imagining it.

He saw the dancers swirling.

He heard the music playing.

He took Susan in his arms and danced.

The Sunday afternoon strollers gazed at John and Susan.
John and Susan never saw them.
They were in memory land.

CHAPTER SIXTY SEVEN

MARCH 2003

LONDON

John Urquhart was doing what he enjoyed most when he died. He was celebrating his retirement from work in an executive box at Arsenal Football Club. On the day he died he was in the box with Sandy Roberts, Leslie Graham and some of Sandy's business colleagues. To add to the exquisite timing of his death he was holding a gin and tonic at the time.

The executive box was not a symbol of a new found status. John Urquhart was as modest in middle-age as he had been when a child roaming the streets of Inverness. The executive box was sponsored by the company that Sandy worked for. It was a perk of the job.

John did not die with a smile on his face. A heart attack is a painful process. He fell to the floor clutching his drink. Despite every effort by Leslie and the paramedics who arrived on the scene ten minutes later there was nothing that could be done.

John's final act took place at the Medway Crematorium six days later. Over one hundred friends and relatives attended the service. A service decided by John months earlier. He was always mindful of the way that his father and brother James had died. He anticipated that when he left there would probably be very little warning.

Despite the religious upbringing that John had in his youth he had declared that his passing would be a day of joy. He had told Susan that when the time came there should be no tears, only memories.

It was the first time Sandy had attended a Humanitarian Service. His eulogy to John paid tribute to a warm family man.

As John moved through the final curtain, the sound of Doris Day filled the Chapel of Rest.

"Que Sera Sera.
whatever will be will be,
the future's not ours to see.
Que Sera Sera".

A week after John Urquhart's funeral service Leslie Graham executed John's last wishes. Susan could not face saying the final good-bye to her John. Sandy was recovering from illness and was unable to travel. It was left to Leslie to carry John's ashes to Inverness.

He scattered John's ashes in the Ness Islands. The wind caught the dust, which settled on the fast running waters. Within moments the last remains of John Urquhart flowed past his place of birth.

After forty seven years of wandering, John Urquhart had finally come home.

The obituary for John Urquhart was published in that week's edition of the Herald. It meant little to most of the townsfolk. But Mary Wilson junior, in her retreat in Drumnadrochit, shed a tear. Violet MacDonald, who read the obituary as she was preparing supper for Billy in their old folks' retirement home, also wept.

They each remembered a young boy who had stolen their hearts.

CHAPTER SIXTY EIGHT

APRIL 2003

KENT, ENGLAND

Two weeks after his cremation John Urquhart's friends held a meeting at his house to discuss the Kessock School re-union which was being held at the New Caley in Inverness the following month. It was unanimously agreed that they should all attend the re-union. As Sandy Roberts pointed out – it would almost certainly be the last opportunity for the old school-friends to get together.

Neither Leslie nor Alison had attended the Kessock School. Alison had never even been in the Ferry area. But it was an opportunity to lay some ghosts to rest. It was an opportunity for Alison to make the peace with her sister Marie.

Alison contacted the organisers of the reunion. They confirmed that Marie Winngate, now known as Lady Castello, would be at the re-union.

CHAPTER SIXTY NINE

MAY 2003

INVERNESS

Retired Police Inspector David Thomson stood at the entrance to the Thistle Lounge in the New Caley Hotel.

He felt it appropriate that he should be there. When he had seen the announcement in the newspaper about a reunion of the former pupils of the Kessock School he knew that Moira would have liked him to be there. Moira had been dead only three months. He missed her more with each passing day.

The Inspector recognised a few of the faces. David Thomson was not too surprised to see Tommy Ross there but he had been surprised to hear that Tommy was working as a financial advisor despite his previous conviction for fraud. Morals and acceptability standards had all but disappeared since the days the Inspector had first pounded the beat.

He recognised the former door-man at the Caley Ballroom. Billy Wilson – was that his name? He had heard that Billy and his wife Violet lived in a home for the elderly because of Billy's dementia. Violet was with Billy, obviously keeping an eye on him.

David Thomson smiled as Sandy Roberts entered the room. He barely knew Sandy. He only knew his name because John Urquhart had given the name "Sandy Roberts" when asked for his identity more than forty years before by a very young Probationary Constable Thomson. It was a pity about Urquhart. He had read his obituary in the Herald only a few weeks before.

Inspector Thomson was brought back to the real world with the realisation that somebody was shaking his hand.

"Well fancy meeting you here. Sorry to hear about Moira.

Sylvia told me all about it. It must be heard for you David."

"I'll be dammed, Jim Smith. What are you up to these days?"

"I'm still cobbling away at the Clach Shoe Repair Shop."

"You still got that mongrel of a dog?"

"Mitch. He's still around, although I had to give him an injection when your leg got in the way of his teeth last year."

"How's Sylvia? I never did get around to thanking her when I saw her at the infirmary. Senior staff nurse isn't she? She's done well Jim, especially for someone who is English."

"I'll give you English. I'm from Yorkshire."

David Thomson turned at the sound of the voice.

"Sylvia Mary Smith! My god you're looking lovelier than ever. I swear you're getting younger each time I see you.

"I'll never know why everyone in this town thinks you have no time for women David Thomson. Moira told me a few things about you."

David Thomson turned away embarrassed. He just hoped that Moira had not said too much about his peculiar habits.

Susan Urquhart was looking around the room. She could see Tommy Burns with his wife Loraine talking to a group of old school friends. Loraine, to Tommy's embarrassment, was telling the story of how Tommy had won the Military Medal in the Falklands War. Judging by the looks on the faces of the listeners, the story was not new to them. Loraine was clearly very proud of her Tommy.

Leslie and Alison Graham were standing beside each other. Alison kept glancing at the door as though half expecting someone to arrive.

More than forty people were assembled in the private lounge. Sandy looked at the group. He recognised about a dozen people. No doubt he had known them all in his childhood. But time had taken its toll.

Inspector Thomson looked out of the lounge window onto the car-park at the rear of the hotel. Below him he could see his son Police Constable Derek Thomson apprehending Ally Henderson. Ally, at the age of seventy eight, was reduced to stealing from parked cars.

"That's my boy," said the proud inspector.

Lady Castello, née Marie Winngate, lay back in her seat on the private jet that was taking her from London to Inverness. She looked out of the cabin window. Despite the time of year there were still pockets of snow on the mountains.

She reflected back on her life. It had certainly been interesting.

Yet so many people had misjudged her.

She had loved all her husbands in her own way. Her first partner Billy Boston had been fun. He was a fool to himself however with his drinking and drugs. She tried in vain to get him to take his blood pressure tablets regularly. He just would not listen. She had felt a great deal of pain when Billy had tragically died.

The accidental deaths of Sir Trevor and Jeffrey were just that. What possessed men of their age to ride a horse and pilot a fast speed boat was beyond her comprehension. She had repeatedly warned them to be careful.

As for Lord Peter Castello. Well, fancy finding Peter naked in the swimming pool with the butler at three o'clock in the morning. She had woken up in the middle of the night. He was not in bed so she went to find him. Until then she had no idea that he and the butler were – she hesitated to use the word – lovers. No wonder the butler was very wary of her afterwards. She and the butler had kept quiet about the incident to protect His Lordship's good name.

She had married her last three husbands because they had given her something she had always lacked. A father figure. How things might have been different if Jocky had been a different type of father. Marie wondered if Alison would be at the reunion. She realised that it was highly unlikely, knowing how snobbish Alison was. But it would be nice to meet her as a sister.

It would be too much to expect little Billy Saunders to be there. It hardly seemed possible that anyone could hold a crush for nearly sixty years. But ever since the VE Day Party in 1945, when they had shared their first childhood kiss, she had awoken every day with Billy on her mind. He was probably married. He could even be dead. What she would give to be young again.

Marie awoke from her reminiscing. The aircraft was

descending.

Billy Saunders was heading for the Kessock School reunion. He had planned to get there in plenty of time but he had been held back at the Auld Lang Syne when a fight had broken out.

He was settled in retirement. It was a total contrast to his active and secret life whilst at Scotland Yard. In retirement he had shaved off his bushy beard and had slimmed down to a respectable fifteen stone. Respectable, that is, for his six foot two inch height. He missed the excitement just a little. Most of the work had been tedious, just surveillance. But that was the downside of being an undercover cop. It was odd that one of his most time consuming cases had been the investigation of one of his primary school friends. Marie Winngate had certainly done a lot with her life. He wondered if she ever suspected that he was nuts about her when they were seven years old. He had got quite excited when he had seen her in the window of the Harbour Inn in 1964, when he had been on the surveillance team keeping an eye on the Algerian Queen. It would be interesting to see if she was at the school re-union.

He sometimes wondered if Marie was guilty of all that was attributed to her. But there never had been enough evidence. Apart that is from the smuggling paperwork he had "mislaid" when they had arrested Eckie Jamieson many years ago. As soon as Billy saw Marie's name on the list of Eckie's contacts he knew he had to destroy the evidence.

He preferred to think that Marie was just another victim of society, the product of a broken home. With a father like Jocky, it was hardly surprising she had gone wrong.

He hoped she would be at the re-union. It was strange. Here he was, still a bachelor at the age of sixty six, and he was having butterflies thinking of Marie Winngate.

The school reunion had been underway an hour when Marie Winngate walked into the room. It was pure coincidence that Billy Saunders walked into the room at the same time.

Billy had the advantage over Marie. He recognised her straight away.

Marie looked at Billy.

It took her ten seconds to realise who he was.

Alison caught Marie's eye from across the room. A small smile flitted from one face to the other.

Alison and Sandy walked across the room.

Alison embraced Marie and then Billy Saunders, in the belief that Marie and Billy were together.

Which, in a way, was appropriate.

It was the early hours of the following day before the reunion finished.

By which time Marie and Billy had discussed the VE Day party of 1945.

CHAPTER SEVENTY

MAY 2003

INVERNESS

Two days after the Kessock School re-union Jocky Winngate was made aware that his two daughters were in town. He was sitting on his favourite stool in the MacEwans Arms when Billy Saunders entered the pub. Jocky agreed to meet Billy for a drink at the Kingsmills Hotel the following day. Marie and Alison would also be there.

It had been sixty five years since Marie and Alison had been conceived.

For the first time in those sixty five years Jocky recalled the name of their mother, the young Health Inspector who had called at Jock's Kitchen on that warm late spring day in 1938.

Karen Forbes.

He could see her now. Fresh faced, officious, but such a wonderful smile.

How would things have turned out if he and Karen had got married when she had told him that she was pregnant? She had wanted to get married. But Jocky was adamant. When he refused to marry her she adopted an air of superiority and decided never to see him again.

Jocky picked up his pint. There was no point in dwelling on the past.

He smiled at the new barmaid.

"I'll have another pint love. Is there anything you fancy?"

Evelyn was not expecting Jocky home for another two hours. She did not mind him being late some nights, especially when she wanted to watch Emmerdale and Holby City.

Jocky watched the door anxiously. Elsie Jamieson had been

visiting the pub on a regular basis. She was sixty years of age and she still carried on as though she was sixteen. Their forty year old son Alastair was the supervisor at Jock's Kitchen. He had arrived back in Inverness with a wealth of catering experience gained in the States. Jocky was aware of four husbands from the Crown district who were keen to have words with his son.

Jocky smiled at the young barmaid again. He was confident that Evelyn would never find out that he had bought his old flat above the fish and chip shop in Grant Street.

After all he was only eighty eight years old.

A man had to have some fun.

CHAPTER SEVENTY ONE

APRIL 2004

BERKSHIRE, ENGLAND

Mrs. Billy Saunders looked out of the window of her manor house. It had been six months since she and Billy had married. It had been a quiet wedding, just a few of their old friends from school days. At their age they were too set in their ways to indulge in lavish wedding receptions.

Their combined business efforts were proceeding smoothly. They had used Billy's contacts in the police and the underworld to raise a considerable amount of money for various charities.

Marie quite liked the idea of taking the American businessmen for a ride. They had made their money through the drug trade.

She was awaiting a telephone call from Billy to tell her that the cash had been handed over, a cool ten million dollars in used bank-notes. Not a bad price for the purchase of Loch Ness. The money was untraceable, which was good news for the restoration fund for the new Kessock School.

The American businessmen would be furious to discover that Loch Ness was not for sale. But it hardly mattered. The F.B.I had been trying to get their hands on the crooks for some time. Billy had told the Feebies about the meeting with the crooks but not about the money. The businessmen were to be arrested as soon as they left the meeting, once the cash was in Billy's hands.

The call from Billy came as Marie was reading that week's edition of The Herald. She still kept in touch with home town activities. Particularly the hatches, matches, and dispatches columns. Just in case her father was up to his old tricks.

Billy confirmed that the money had been received, and that he and the Nelson brothers were on their way back to England.

Marie replaced the telephone receiver.

She was missing Billy.

For the first time in her life she was really content.

Meanwhile, back in Inverness, Police Constable Derek Thomson and his father, retired Inspector David Thomson, was checking the old file on Marie Winngate.

Billy Saunders was Marie's fifth husband. They had been married six months.

P.C. Derek Thomson decided to keep an eye on the marriage.

Just in case.